MYRIAD

THE RISE OF A SUPERHERO

CREATED & WRITTEN BY
DON RILING

To a Myriad of Adventures!

INSPIRED BY
MICHAEL HAMM

xoxo

Dedicated to **Michael Hamm**
For helping me through the pandemic and
providing the inspiration for this story.
A true hero in and out of costume. Thank you
for reigniting my lifelong desire to write.

CONTENTS

PROJECT PENDANT

Marcel bent over the coffee-table in his tiny studio apartment in Greenwich Village. It was hot and sticky outside, even for June in New York City. When he had returned to his apartment an hour ago, the mercury had already risen to 94 degrees, and the air was thick with humidity.

"No matter," he mumbled to himself, "I've *got* to get this piece finished for tonight."

Marcel had a special gift for making beautiful jewelry. Normally, he created his adornments for some of his fellow drag queen friends and sometimes he would show up at a Saturday market in the Village to sell pieces for extra cash. This particular gem he was finishing, however, was to be for him.

This was not going to be just any usual piece of jewelry, and in truth he didn't even know if there was any merit to what he was trying to do. Would it actually have any power? Or would it just be symbolic? Marcel wasn't sure of the answer but given the nature of what was likely to happen tonight, he knew he would need all the help he could get.

He looked down at his latest creation. Originally, he'd intended for it to be a broach. But once he started formulating his idea for it, he opted instead to make it a pendant to hang on a choker. Usually for anything like a pendant Marcel would begin with a one-inch circular tray made of zinc alloy. Given his height (6'2"—quite tall and imposing in heels for a drag queen!), he wanted to instead make this a clear statement piece. He'd had the pendant tray specially made in the two-inch diameter he desired. While most queens favored gold, he much preferred silver. Fashioning the incredibly thin silver wire to separate the individual spaces in the pendant was an exercise in patience. Once he finished the wiring, there was an inner circle a half-inch from the outer diameter. The ring surrounding the inner circle was divided into seven equal (almost) sections. These would be for the individual colors of the rainbow.

At first, he wasn't sure what he would do to imbue this piece with something near and dear to his heart. But when Judy had died just six days ago—on June 22, 1969—his heart had broken. Tears welled just at the thought of her, and how much she'd yearned for acceptance and understanding her entire life. Now that she was gone (far too soon from this world and his life), the symbolism of the rainbow from the song forever linked to her felt not only the right design element for his pendant, but also a way to honor Judy's importance in his life. She loved her gay followers, and they loved her in return. Plus, it just felt important for her to be present in some small way tonight.

Marcel temporarily sat down the pendant, rubbing his fingertips. They were sore from the painstaking wiring work, but he still had more to do. He glanced over at the note that had been slipped under his door that morning from Benny, the manager of the Stonewall Inn. The note simply read: *Tonight we say enough. I hope Melodie will be in attendance.*

Stonewall had become a home for Marcel and several other fellow drag queens, never mind the entire gay community. As one of the

only bars where they felt safe to gather, its haven was of critical importance. It didn't stop the near weekly raids of the place by the police. It
seemed they were happening even more frequently over the past several months. While the offense used to be a public display to show city
officials that the cops were doing something to *keep the gays in check,*
the raids of late had become more violent with more patron arrests.
Not only were these attacks an invasion of their safe space, the knowledge that the police were taking money from Benny weekly in order to
keep the bar open (they currently had no liquor license) was infuriating.
Just two weeks ago, Stonewall was given the news that the bribe would
increase by another $500.

The fact the cops were demanding more illegal money to keep
the Inn open along with the increasing raids was enough. Tonight a raid
was expected; tonight they would rise up and take a stand. No more
would they flee and meekly cower in the corners of the bar until the
attack was over or be singled out and arrested. Tonight was going to
end differently.

TWO

NEW YORK
... I'M IN YOU

 Michael swiped the card key on the hotel room's sensor pad and opened the door to his room at Hyperion Hotel. Relieved that it worked this time around, he lugged his suitcase inside, dropped his backpack and kicked off his sneakers, then plopped onto the bed. It had been a long day of travel from Halifax, given that the flight to New York had been delayed over two hours and he hadn't found that out until he'd already arrived at Halifax Stanfield International. He could have used the extra few hours of sleep, given that the flight was originally scheduled for a 7:15 a.m. departure.

When he finally got to the hotel in Hell's Kitchen, he was ready for a hot shower and a good meal. That goal was annoyingly delayed by the first round of room keys not working. Granted, the guy who checked him in was quite cute and rather flirty, but his ability to flirt and do his job correctly apparently was more than the Canadian could hope for. *Ah well ...* he thought, *cute and efficient don't always go hand in hand.*

Now that he'd had a chance to stretch out on the bed, he could take in the room. It was more spacious than he expected and well appointed, which was a lovely surprise. Given that the New York City Comic-Con unexpectedly reached out to help with air and hotel to the Con, he was expecting something a little sparser.

This was his first Comic-Con in a while. In fact, Michael really hadn't considered going to this convention, given he had just traveled to Florida two weeks earlier for a much-needed Disney escape. But it was 2022 and, since most of the issues surrounding the pandemic were now settled, Michael had resolved to immerse himself back into the public part of his cosplay career. While there were some commitments he wasn't really keen to fulfill that the Con required in exchange for the travel and lodging support, he nevertheless had accepted the offer. It was a good way to help forge ahead into Con participation. Plus, he loved New York City.

First requirement: a good long shower. He slid off the bed, stripped off his clothes and opened his suitcase. He pulled out his toiletries and headed to the bathroom. The walk-in shower was spacious, and the water pressure was strong.

Toweling off, he wiped away the fog on the mirror and gazed at his reflection. "Ugh, I need a haircut." Michael had intended to get his hair handled before the trip, but the move to his new apartment (another reason he'd considered declining the Con invite) had taken up nearly every spare minute before the trip. Plus, he'd spent an inordinate amount of time finishing his new Arsenal costume to give him an extra hero to debut at the Con.

He raked his fingers through his hair, gave his best effort to make it look good, and then decided he should take a few impromptu bathroom shots for his Fandom page. Living this life meant being constantly aware of any good opportunities to create content to share with his supporters and on social media. Plus, he'd been working out and paying painful attention to his diet the last ten days to ... be impressive when he showed up for the Con. He needed to take every chance he could to capitalize on his hard work.

He reviewed the shots on his iPhone, chose two for Fandom (one that particularly showed off his tight ass and flexed thigh), then finished getting ready. Choosing to unpack the rest of his suitcase later, he pulled out a fresh pair of undies, jeans, tee and ball cap and looked on his phone for a close spot to get a haircut. After considering a couple of places, he booked an online appointment. He had two hours to kill— plenty of time to head out and explore Times Square and find someplace to grab a bite to eat.

He left his hotel room and headed for the elevator. Pressing the button to head for the lobby, he grinned as he thought to himself, *Heads up, New York! Michael Hamm is ready to be in you.*

LET'S GET ENCHANTED

Marcel woke up with a start. He had finished the pendant and slid it on the perfect sterling silver chain, then decided to lie back on the sofa and rest his eyes. He wasn't expecting his entire body to rest right along with them! He looked over at the kitchen clock: 6:43 p.m. "Fuck!" he cried out. "How's a queen supposed to get ready in under three hours?" Plus, he still had to place the finishing touch—or rather incantation—on his new pendant.

Adrenaline kicked in and he was in and out of the shower in record time. Fortunately, he already knew what he was going to wear tonight—a hot little bright blue sequin minidress. It had a plunging neckline that would highlight his new pendant splendidly, and he had chosen perfect hammered silver hoops to go with the look. Given that he wasn't entirely sure how the night would go, he chose a chunky heel that was not as high as some of the others he might normally wear.

The tucking, foundation and the finish makeup ... well, that was going to take some time. After all, Melodie Monnaie couldn't show up for tonight's event without putting her best look forward. Whether onstage or not, there simply *must* be a show.

Once he sat down in front of the mirror, he went into muscle memory makeup mode. He really *could* probably do this with his eyes closed, but tonight wasn't the time to experiment with that. Looking at his reflection, he proceeded to enhance his eyes with the longest eyelashes he had, and metallic indigo eye shadow to pop with the mini-dress and his new pendant.

The pendant … *yes!* He undid the clasp on the silver chain and wrapped it around his neck. The size was dramatic—exactly what he envisioned. Each color of the rainbow was represented in the outer ring with the crushed gemstones he had painstakingly glued within each wire-framed space. Crushed cubic zirconia filled the middle to give the pendant a flash of silver. And—dead in the center—a very special jewel— the blood-red garnet passed down to each generation of his family from his Grandmama Marie du Monde. It was said the garnet held dormant magic. Tonight, he would try to revive it.

He thought if there was ever a night he could use some extra protection, this would be it.

He pulled his family photo album from the bottom drawer of his vanity and opened it to the first page. He removed the daguerreotype which pictured Grandmama Marie taken some time in the late 1800s just after her arrival in Louisiana. She was a striking woman—one of the first French Creole of his lineage to travel to America and settle in New Orleans: high cheekbones, coffee-colored skin, piercing eyes, and impressive cleavage. Even though the daguerreotype was monochrome, he could feel her amber-colored eyes staring right through him. And she wore the very garnet in a formidable ring that was now affixed to the center of his pendant.

He flipped over the image of Marie. The words written on the reverse were so faded they could now barely be read. It took a very bright light and magnifying glass to reveal the phrase. It was said that these very words could imbue a precious stone with power to protect the wearer. Indeed, it was rumored his Grandmama Marie had visited a witch in one of the bayous around New Orleans shortly after her arrival, seeking a way to protect her family as they embarked on a new life in America.

The tale: For one piece of silver, the witch agreed to enchant her ring—the most precious and valuable thing she owned. Grandmama Marie pulled the new daguerreotype just finished from her satchel, handing it to the enchantress. She requested the witch write on the back the exact words that were to safeguard her family for generations to come.

The witch—called Septima—lit a candle, placed it in the center of a small round table, and sat cross-legged on the floor. At Septima's bidding, Marie took off her ring and handed it to the enchantress, who then removed the scarf from her head and wrapped it around the piece of jewelry. She passed the scarf over the candle in a circular motion as she uttered the following in French:

> *"Donnez-moi de la force, de la vitesse,*
> *de la sagesse, du courage et de l'orgueil.*
> *Je suis une myriade de magie."*

Once Septima had finished the enchantment, a rush of wind blew out the candle.

"There … it is done," said the witch, unwrapping the scarf. She grabbed Marie's hand and returned the garnet ring to her finger, then presented the palm of her other hand to Marie, who placed the promised silver in the witch's hand. Then, Septima carefully wrote the spell on the reverse of Marie's daguerreotype and handed it back to her.

Those were the freshly translated words that Marcel now looked at on the piece of paper he had unfolded. While he hailed from a Creole heritage, his ability to speak French was wanting. He had asked his next-door neighbor Fran to enlist the aid of her boyfriend Frank (yes, *really*, they were a couple with the names Fran and Frank!) to translate the phrase into English. He just hoped the translation would have the same magical effect the French enchantment was reported to have that Septima had uttered nearly two centuries ago.

He placed his fingers over the pendant, resting the tip of his ring finger on top of the garnet. He stared into the mirror, and in his best mystical voice, read:

*"Bestow upon me strength, speed, wisdom, courage, and pride.
I am a myriad of magic."*

He continued to gaze in the mirror at the pendant once he'd completed speaking—nothing. "Hmm," he mused. Should something have happened—something to give him even a slight indication that the enchantment had worked? Not getting any literal satisfaction from the spell was disappointing.

He looked down at the scrap of paper again, double checking that he had indeed uttered the words in the correct sequence. He was sure he had. The last sentence of the spell seemed the most important piece of the incantation. Inspiration struck him, and he removed the silver choker from around his neck and flipped the pendant over. He found a soldering iron that he sometimes used when crafting jewelry.

Very carefully he used the hot iron tip to inscribe the word *Myriad* on its silver surface, and then returned the choker to its place around his neck.

What the hell, he thought. Whether it worked or not, the pendant would help embolden him for whatever happened at the Stonewall Inn tonight.

UNEXPECTED PLANS

Michael got back to his hotel room, energized by the rhythm of New York City. Just walking the streets, riding the subway, visiting Broadway ... all gave him a lighter spring in his step. The fresh haircut certainly felt good too.

He opened the door and noticed a big basket sitting on his bed with a tiny envelope attached. It was filled with fresh fruit—apples, oranges, bananas, and more. *What a nice surprise!* he thought. He sat on the bed and pulled the note off the basket and opened it. When he read the contents, he groaned, "Ohh ... what a nice surprise." He was hoping to just chill out tonight and get a good night's rest before embarking on his event commitments. Alas, the note dashed those hopes. It read:

> *Michael! We're so thrilled you're here for the New York City Comic-Con! Tonight, we're hosting a special private event for some of the guests involved in the Con, along with some fans who have helped underwrite our return after the pandemic. It starts at 9:00 p.m. at the Stonewall Inn. Look forward to seeing you there!*

The note was signed by Ned, who had been his contact for the New York City Comic-Con.

He lay back on the bed and crammed one of the pillows under his head. Now that he had a moment to think about it, he vaguely recalled Ned emailing him about the potential for this appearance at the Inn, but that was all he remembered.

He glanced over at the basket again and saw there was a second larger envelope sticking out from under the bananas. He pulled the packet out. Inside was the full itinerary for his time at the Con, and the first thing on the timeline was tonight's get together.

He sighed. "Okay … well shit—let's figure out who will make an appearance tonight." He had been told they would love to see him in some of his most popular looks for the convention—the ones that were iconically tied to Michael Hamm, the pro-cosplayer: Spider-Man, Nightwing, Superboy were specifically called out. He had packed all three of those in their latest incarnations, along with his recently revealed classic Cyclops.

Guess it's time to unpack the suitcase and make a decision. He pulled it up onto the bed and started to unzip it. He had packed a good amount, and the suitcase sprung open the minute it was fully unzipped. Folding the upper half of the suitcase over onto the bed, he pulled out each costume he'd carefully packed in their individual bags. Well … he was in New York City, home of Spider-Man. But his new Nightwing costume was demanding its debut and, given that the Stonewall Inn was a gay bar, he felt the sexual vibe of Dick Grayson's hero identity would be a hit.

He laughed out loud at the thought. The last thing he ever truly wanted or gave any thought to when he started his cosplay career was how fans would view him sexually. As an introvert, it was one of those things he found the most awkward and challenging. It took him a number of years to even *start* feeling less self-conscious about it, and he knew he truly never would totally embrace what others saw in him ... in *that* way. And, depending on who the fan was the attention either made him feel quite flattered ... or a little on the *creepy* side. He prayed tonight there would be more flattery and less creepy.

It was already 7:30. He decided to head up to the fitness center for a brief party pump, another quick shower, and then he would get geared and ready for the journey downtown to Greenwich.

FIVE

A Riotous Affair

When Melodie arrived, the bar was packed. And, given that the temperature outside was still 80 degrees, it was damn hot too. She gave Hugh, the doorman, a quick peck on the cheek as she breezed past. Melodie was well known at the Stonewall, confirmed by the cheers and greetings upon her arrival.

She claimed her reserved seat at the bar and greeted Tony. The bartender was looking particularly hunky: bare chested in his leather harness and skintight black leather pants. He was from Georgia, and his southern accent made Melodie's juices flow. "Hello darlin'," he greeted her, "what's your pleasure tonight?"

"What would be my *pleasure* is unfortunately not on the menu, so I'll settle for a dirty martini ... *Sir.*"

Tony laughed and turned to make Melodie's drink. The drag queen in turn ogled his ass in that skintight leather, making her all the more thirsty.

She'd barely had a sip of her drink when Benny emerged from his office at the back of the bar. He strode over to Melodie, gave her a kiss and a hug, and said, "Hey, given what might happen tonight, I think it's important to get some of the regulars together and take a photo of all of you. Are you up for it?"

Melodie laughed. "Sweetie, when have you *ever* known me to turn down a photo op? Where would you like to take the pictures?"

"I think here in front of the bar with Tony, so we get the full feel of the Inn," Benny replied.

"Sounds perfect. I'll get some folks together and we'll be ready in ten minutes."

Melodie tasked herself with gathering some of the regulars Benny would surely want included in the shot: A couple of the other drag queens who performed there on Tuesday night along with him; Jake and Jeremy, an older couple who'd been together for thirty-three years; two of the hot young barboys, Bernardo and Theo. They joined Tony and Benny along with Glo, the bar matriarch. At seventy-three, she was truly the heart and soul of the Stonewall.

After about ten minutes of fussing, checking makeup, tweaking exposed nipples and cheeks (and maybe an ass grab or two that had nothing to do with the photo shoot), Benny had everyone positioned to his satisfaction. Thinking ahead, he had contacted someone from *The Daily News* about what might occur tonight, and they had sent one of their photographers, Danny, to be on hand to report anything. Danny took a number of good shots of the group, who then retreated to their normal hangouts in the bar.

The evening progressed as it usually did, and it seemed perhaps the night was going to be uneventful after all. It was now after 1:00 a.m. But little did any of the patrons know that a number of the undercover officers had managed to successfully gain entry earlier. They had tipped off the squad that was ready to raid the Inn.

At about 1:20 a.m., Deputy Inspector Pine—who normally commandeered the raids for that ass Mayor Wagner who ordered them—stared down Hugh, pushed the doors to the Stonewall Inn open and shouted, "Police! We're taking the place. Everyone stay where you are."

The crowd in the bar momentarily tensed, then everything went crazy and chaos ensued. Even though these raids were commonplace, there was never any way to really prepare for what might happen. Still, the bar crowd went about doing what they normally did when a raid occurred: illegal drugs were flushed or concealed, couples previously entwined in dance separated, anyone revealing anything considered indecent buttoned and zipped up. The black lights were turned off and instead the bar was flooded with white light. Some tried to slip out the back or make their way past the officers through the front doors, but both were now blocked.

No one at the Stonewall wanted to end up in a jail cell if they could prevent it, or injured—or both.

Melodie retreated to the corner of the bar near the pool table. In past raids, she had noted that this particular area seemed to remain off the policemen's radar when they pushed their way in and began their harassment. She took a good swig of her martini, perched herself on the barstool, and waited.

"Everyone line up," one of the officers barked. "We want to see IDs, now."

Glo, kaftan flowing, marched right up to the officer that gave the order, and said, "I want to know why you've barged your way in here and ruined a perfectly good night for people minding their own business and not hurting anyone!"

The officer looked down at Glo and gave her a grim smirk. "You had best get in line, sweetheart, and do as you're told." He gave her a slight shove, enraging Tony, who quickly sprung from behind the bar and wedged himself between Glo and the officer.

"How *dare you* push a seventy-year-old woman! Did your mother not teach you anything about respect?"

The officer wasn't having any of it. He grabbed hold of Tony's harness and said, "I don't have any respect for anyone like *YOU*." He backhanded Tony, which sounded like a thunderclap in the starkly lit bar.

And that was it. Everyone began shouting and fists started flying, people were pushed to the ground, billy clubs came out, and suddenly it turned into a riot.

Melodie's hopes that her little corner would remain off the police radar were dashed. In fact, one of the officers made his way to that very corner and grabbed her arm. "Come with me, *miss*."

Melodie jerked her arm out of the policeman's grasp. "Get your hands off me!" she screamed.

The cop then hauled off and slapped her and Melodie's raven-colored wig flew off her head. As she fell to the floor, ears ringing, the cop tried to grab her again. Sadly, the only thing he was able to grasp was her new silver choker with its enchanted pendant. As he ripped it from Melodie's neck, the chain broke. Then a flash of light blinded the officer, who yelled in surprise and pain. The policeman's eyes widened at the light emanating from the pendant and the resulting shock, then uttered a groan before crumpling to the floor.

Stunned by what just happened, Melodie realized the spell must have worked. Looking at the officer lying beside her, she needed to get the pendant away from him. It took some work get it out of his grasp. The shock appeared to have partially paralyzed the cop and his fingers were curled tightly around the pendant. But after about thirty seconds, Melodie prevailed, and prying it from his fist, she reclaimed the charmed piece of jewelry.

Then she panicked. What if someone saw what happened and tied it to the pendant and ultimately to her? She had to hide it—and fast. Looking behind her, she spied a floorboard at the base of the wall in the corner that appeared loose. She pulled a nail file from her purse and worked it into the space between the boards. After some jiggling, the board gave way and revealed a small space underneath. She quickly placed the pendant inside. Before putting the board back in place, she whispered the word she had inscribed on the back of the pendant in her apartment earlier that night ... *"Myriad."*

She replaced the floorboard and looked around to see if anyone was paying her any mind. In the chaos, no one had even noticed (or cared) that the officer had collapsed. Then, before she realized what was happening, another flash of light filled the bar.

And Melodie Monnaie disappeared.

SIX

A NIGHT FOR NIGHTWING

Michael pulled his ball cap lower over his face, stepped out of the car, and quickly thanked the driver, who stared at him. It was always far more convenient to head to events in costume, but it could nevertheless be awkward and embarrassing. His jacket helped conceal Nightwing somewhat, but the way the costume's spandex clung to the lower half of his body left nothing to the imagination. He wasn't one to blush, thank God. Otherwise, every appearance he did would feature a non-stop, beet red flush to his cheeks.

As he walked up to the Stonewall Inn, he saw a poster near the entry with his publicity shot along with several other pro-cosplayers apparently scheduled that night. He was the main guest, so his face was more prominently displayed; his name was emblazoned across the flyer under the event title—awkward and embarrassing as well.

He was greeted immediately by Ned as he entered the bar. He was a thirty-something fanboy who was clearly geeking out over his success at persuading Michael Hamm to re-emerge and make his first Con appearance since the pandemic. "Michael!" Surprisingly, he grabbed the

20

cosplayer's spandex-clad left hand in his own and shook it. He must have taken note that the guest star was a southpaw. Well played. "It's so terrific to have you here! What can I get you to drink? Are you hungry? What do you need?"

Taking a deep calming breath, Michael smiled an impish grin and replied, "It's so great to be here! I appreciate the invitation. I'm perfectly happy with just water at the moment. But I do need to know where I can set up and finish putting on the other pieces of my costume and mask up."

"Right away," Ned answered. "I've got a spot for you in the manager's office ready with a mirror, and there's a bathroom right next door."

After an introduction to the bar's manager, Jason, he was ushered into the office. The door shut, and he sighed in relief. Michael had forty-five minutes before he had to be out front, onstage and turn on the Hammy hero charm.

He opened his backpack and pulled out the rest of the costume to complete his latest Nightwing: utility belt, motorbike style leg bag, armguards, shoulder armor, and sport bike gloves. And, of course, the all-important mask, adhesive, and eye black. Originally, he'd planned to put the shin guards and boots on once he got to the Inn, but they were so bulky, he'd decided to wear them. Michael had been so focused on completing his Arsenal costume before leaving home that he hadn't finished the back holster he was working on for Nightwing's Escrima sticks. But he had the sticks ready for the purpose of this appearance, so it would still feel complete.

He unzipped the costume at the forearms to slide off the spandex gloves so he could prep his eyes and don the mask. Getting the eye black exactly right to look perfect with the mask took some diligence, but it was something he was used to doing by now, and he finished the task in less than five minutes. He prepped the back of the mask with the adhesive and pressed it on. This was the boring part—sitting around not moving or doing anything while the adhesive had a chance to set. There was nothing more annoying than an unintentional unmasking due to adhesive failure. That would *definitely* not be a thing tonight.

When enough time had gone by, he checked it in the mirror. Awesome! It not only looked great, but his fresh haircut was on point. So far, so good.

Next, he fastened on the belt he'd partially crafted, and then strapped on the leg bag, similar to those used by sport motor bikers. One of the bonuses of the bag—it was a great place to keep a few things: ChapStick, breath mints, and his wallet were always within reach. One of the *unintentional* bonuses—the upper strap wrapped around the top of his right thigh just under the ass cheek and made it pop. That Avenger might have America's ass, but Michael Hamm's Nightwing had Canada's ass!

He affixed the shoulder armor in place and then positioned the armguards. Once everything felt right, he pulled a curl of hair down so it fell in front of his forehead, then looked at himself in the mirror making various expressions to ensure the mask stayed in place. Satisfied, he pulled the spandex gloves back on and zipped the costume's forearms, then slid the moto-style gloves on and pulled the Velcro straps tight to keep them snug and firmly in place. The gloves helped accentuate the motorbike themed look of his latest version of this superhero.

He checked the front, side, and rear views of Nightwing. Everything was looking good. Just a few shots for his Fandom page and he'd be ready to greet the fans. (Weird to have fans, but it was the truth.)

After about ten minutes, there was a knock on the door. "Michael— are you ready—we sure are!"

Michael gritted his teeth and opened the door. "I'm ready!"

Ned gasped. "Wow ... you certainly *are*. Did I mention that Nightwing is my favorite character?"

The Canadian thought to himself, *Well, I certainly know now.*

He grabbed his backpack which held his Escrima sticks and headed down the hallway with Ned.

SEVEN

WHO WAS THAT MASKED MAN?

For the most part, things were going quite well. Michael and the other cosplay guests each had their respective tables. His was in the corner near the pool table. Fans stopped by with one of his pics or the tees he sold online to be signed, and there were photo ops galore. After several minutes, Michael's initial insecurity about doing something so publicly drifted away and he settled into his pseudo-celebrity role.

Nearly forty-five minutes into his guest stint, he regrettably realized he drank more water than he should have, and had to take a break to pee. Signaling to Ned, he left it to him to inform those waiting in line that he would be back in ten minutes.

Fortunately, he had the partial costume disrobe down. Once in the bathroom, he maneuvered into a stall and proceeded to take care of business. As he was getting his costume back in proper order, he thought the floor under him was vibrating. *Is this really happening?* he thought in a panic. Earthquakes were not a normal New York City occurrence. He grabbed the stall door handle. *He was right.* Things were vibrating.

What to do? He left the bathroom and as he hurried down the hall, the vibration subsided. *Well, what the hell?* he thought. *Am I crazy?* He opted not to say anything and returned to his celebrity table in the corner of the bar.

The next fan in line—a rather cute guy who told Michael his name was also Mike—greeted him shyly and confessed how he was such a big fan and absolutely a Nightwing lover. He only wished Michael had his Escrima sticks, as he would love a photo of Nightwing's arms wrapped around him holding the glowing sticks.

The sticks! What a dummy. They were in his backpack and he'd intended to pull them out for photos.

Michael grinned at the fanboy. "Guess what? I actually have them right here in my backpack. Let me grab them and we'll get some fun shots." The other Mike was delighted.

He knelt down to unzip his pack lying in the corner on the floor. Just as he started to open it, he saw what looked like a bright white light framing one of the floorboards near the wall. *What the hell is happening to me? First vibrating, now this? Am I hallucinating?* He closed his eyes tight for a moment (he couldn't rub them with the eye black and mask), then slowly opened them back up. Well … something was up. The glow was still there.

"Everything okay?" the other Mike asked.

"Uhh … yep, I'll be right there," he responded. Michael had a small flathead screwdriver in the side pocket of his backpack. It was slim enough to wedge into the groove between the floorboards. He slid it in and gently pried the board up. The minute he did so, the glow subsided. But what was this? Inside he found a round piece of jewelry—a belt buckle, or something. He pulled it out and took a closer look. Even in the indirect light, he could see the rainbow colors of the jeweled piece shimmering.

He stood up to get a better look at his discovery, and realized it was a pendant with a loop on the top to slide a chain into.

As he flipped the pendant over, the floor began vibrating under his feet—far more than it had in the bathroom. Then he read the word on the back of the pendant out loud—"*Myriad*"—and in that exact moment there was also a sudden blast. The old boiler in the restaurant next door had been the source of the vibration, and now it had just exploded, causing the wall on the opposite side of the bar to blast open and erupt into flames.

Michael felt a rush of warmth and tingling engulf his entire body. This was not a result of the explosion; it had something to do with the pendant. He looked at the mirror behind the bar across from him. What he saw was unbelievable. His image as Nightwing was *CHANGING*. A glow similar to the one he'd seen spilling from around the floorboard now enveloped him. And, as the light swallowed him, he felt his Nightwing costume going through a metamorphosis. Once the glow dissipated, he looked again at his reflection in the barroom mirror. He was still costumed, but the hero in the reflection was someone different—someone new and unrecognizable.

As all this was happening everything to Michael appeared to move in slow motion, including the effects of the explosion. He realized in a split second that everyone needed to get to safety—fast.

That's when it struck him that nothing else was moving in slow motion. He looked down at his hands—which were now framed in black leather gloves that went up the length of his forearms—and they were vibrating. Michael grasped that the feeling of slow-motion movement was exactly what happened to his comic book heroes when they possessed the power of superspeed, just like Flash or Quicksilver.

What the holy hell, Hammy? Did he suddenly have—superspeed? There was only one way to find out. He looked at the other Mike, who had ducked under his celebrity table for cover. In a flash, he scooped up the fanboy and was outside with him in a nanosecond. Both were now standing on the sidewalk across the street from the Stonewall Inn.

Wow-wow-wow-wow-wow—what the fuck is going on? Michael thought, but there was no time for figuring that out. If he had super-speed, he needed to get everyone out of that bar to safety as quickly as he could before the full brunt of the explosion peaked.

Instincts he never knew he had took over and he was off, thinking rapidly how speedsters used their powers to rescue bystanders.

By the time a minute had passed, Michael had managed to deposit every patron of the Stonewall Inn and the restaurant next door safely out of harm's way. As the bar goers, coughing and stumbling, struggled to fig-ure out what had just happened to them, the cosplayer turned his atten-tion to the fire. Racing around the flames from the explosion in rapid circles, he created a vacuum to extinguish the flames and stop the flying debris. Within minutes, the whole thing was over.

Michael raced to the opposite side of the street where he had taken the survivors. They were all talking amongst themselves, trying to comprehend how they'd miraculously avoided the explosion and were still alive.

Michael spotted Ned in the crowd, whose stunned gaze was directed Michaels's way. "Look!" Ned cried out, and several of the attend-ees near him turned to face this new superhero. "I think he's the one who saved us! But who is he? Who is THAT masked man?"

Still reeling, one thing Michael knew for sure: he had to get out of there and figure out what the heck just happened. And how the holy hell he had just managed to ... *super.*

EIGHT

UM ...
WHAT NOW?

 Michael sped back to Hell's Kitchen and zoomed up the side of Hyperion Hotel. When he reached the twelfth floor, he used his new superspeed and vibrated through the walls and into room #1220. He came to a stop in front of the full-length mirror in his room. He was only slightly out of breath after all that! But, when he looked at his reflection, the image he saw did truly take his breath away.

During his career, Michael Hamm had the good fortune to take on the persona of many of his favorite superheroes. From an incredibly early age he'd yearned to be Spider-Man or Batman's sidekick Robin. Halloween was a treat, as he could dress up in something that loosely resembled his childhood comic heroes and escape.

As he got older, he recognized that his secret fantasies were best explored reading his comics in the privacy of his own home. The kids at school didn't really understand, and he'd felt uneasy sharing his passion. In retrospect, it was at that time in his life when he acknowledged the introvert part of his personality. He decided back then that some things are simply better left to a secret space.

Then, Michael discovered Comic-Cons—a wonderful thing! Here people with a love for comics, sci-fi, Japanese animation, video games and more would gather. He'd been mesmerized by the attendees that dressed as their favorite superheroes at the first one he attended. Some just wore schlocky getups that were fun or tongue-in-cheek, yet others were decked out in full-on costumes close to authentically bringing their superheroes to life. He'd had a titillating thought—creating his version of Spider-Man, Robin, or another of his faves and attending a convention. But he just couldn't get up the nerve.

It wasn't until he went to a Halloween party one year in costume that someone urged him to get into serious cosplay and go to a Con as one of his favorite characters. With a bit of help, he constructed his first look and braved attending a convention in costume. After that, he was hooked.

As time wore on, he embarked on an actual cosplay career doing what he loved, designing numerous costumes, some made just for him to his exact measurements. Sometimes he looked in the mirror wearing a custom-made costume for the first time and could not believe how lucky he felt. Doing this for a living and ending up with a bit of notoriety had been astounding.

Today, as he studied his reflection, was surreal. There were several custom-made costumes that made him giddy when he put them on for the first time. Even his new Nightwing that he'd worn to the Stonewall Inn gave him such joy, as it fit perfectly. But the costume he wore now—he'd never had anything fit him like this, ever.

Cosplay was a lot of fun and he loved it. This ... THIS was on another level altogether.

This costume fit him flawlessly, giving him a new appreciation for his dedicated workouts the past few weeks.

He turned on the light to get a better look at—*his?*—costume. Black leather boots hugged his calves which gently peaked in the front. The gloves had similar peaks just beyond his elbows. The bodysuit was a combination of bright blue and silver. A mid-width black leather belt framed his waist and dropped in the center to accentuate his torso's V. The mask was also black, stylized a bit like a Robin or Nightwing mask but with a subtle difference to the overall silhouette. It was finished with a sliver of silver accent. There was a stylized *M* encircled by a ring centered over his left pec. Behind the *M* a diagonal slash of deep glowing red made the emblem pop. It was the only spot on the costume that didn't feature the otherwise silver/blue/black color scheme.

He turned to get a side view. *Damn!* he mused. Somehow this costume hugged his ass making it pop, similar to the way his Nightwing leg belt had.

He turned forward again and took in this new version of himself. *Wonder what this would look like with a cape?* he thought.

What the …? Michael stared at his reflection as a glow started to envelop him the same way it had back in the Stonewall Inn. He watched as a cape sprung from his shoulders and flowed down mid-calf, and then the glow faded. The cape was silver with a black lining; the bottom rose to a slight peak in the center to match the peaks of the boots and gloves. He turned around to look at the back. Two thin diagonal black stripes were on either side of a bright blue stripe between them. Between his shoulder blades was a similar emblem like the one on his chest.

"I can't believe this," he said aloud. "I mean … how did this happen?"

He stared down at his gloved hands, attempting to move them at superspeed like he had back at the Inn when he first realized he had somehow gained the ability to do so, but there was no satisfaction. "Hmm … well, this is all … *extra*."

He slowly walked over and sat on the bed. Draping his cape to the right, he crossed his legs. Michael rested his back on the padded headboard. He sat there for several minutes, his mind racing. He went over the events of the past few hours, retracing what happened at the Stonewall. His thoughts eventually brought him back to the mysterious pendant he'd found just before the blast.

Where was the pendant? He could see it in his mind as if he still had it in his grasp.

The word on the back—when he had said that word, that's when this all began. *That pendant must have something to do with his new-found abilities and this costume.*

Closing his eyes, he whispered the word again: "*Myriad.*"

The warm tingling he'd felt the first time overtook him again, and he opened his eyes to the bright light surrounding him once more. When the glow dissipated, he was back in his Nightwing costume. At the foot of the bed, his backpack with the rest of his stuff and his Escrima sticks had reappeared. And he clutched the pendant in his left hand again.

He sat bolt upright, adrenaline hitting him in a way he'd never experienced. His life had irrevocably changed today.

And all he could think was, *Umm ... what now?*

NINE

SÉANCE IN NEW ORLEANS

After nearly a half-hour of frustrating hunting, Travis finally found a parking spot not too far off Bourbon Street. He hated coming to this part of the city for any reason, and he couldn't understand why his mother insisted on this annual silly pursuit. However, his southern deference to his parental units and guilt made him succumb to his mother's wishes to meet her in the French Quarter. His only reward would be beignets at Café du Monde afterward. His mouth watered at the mere thought.

He walked the seven blocks to his destination—the tiny storefront on Bienville Street. Glancing at the lettering on the window, he winced as he read: *Forays into the Other Dimension*. Below the shop's name was listed its proprietress, *Madame Beatriz, Spiritualist*. With a sigh he muttered, "Alrighty then," and opened the door.

His mother was already inside, seated on one of the faded upholstered chairs in the little waiting area. It was dimly lit, no doubt to hide the aging of most of the furnishings and the striped, burgundy wallpaper. The ceiling was lit with small pinpoints of light to mimic a night sky.

A table sat off to one side with a very old commercial coffeepot, carafe with hot water, and a selection of herbal teas. He noted his mother had partaken, no doubt sipping some of the lemon zinger she preferred.

His mother, Eugenia, was obsessed with mysterious disappearances and the unknown. Travis often came home from clubbing on the weekend to find her planted in front of the TV, sometimes with a pint of dulce de leche ice cream. Her eyes were usually fixated on the screen, watching with rapt attention as details unfolded surrounding some true crime or unsolved mystery.

Her obsession stemmed from her teen years when Eugenia's mother—his grandma Celeste—had shared the story of Eugenia's Uncle Marcel with her for the first time. His mother had been fascinated by Marcel's unexplained disappearance the night of the riot at the Stonewall Inn back in 1969. Having a relative vanish who was not only part of the beginning of the Gay Rights Movement but did so in glitter and heels felt daring and rife with mystery.

Their family knew Marcel had been there the night of the riot. After his disappearance, the Inn's bartender—Tony—had sent Celeste a note to say how sorry he was that her brother was nowhere to be found. He had enclosed the photo taken by The Daily News depicting Travis's great uncle sitting in a mini-dress, heels and choker, legs crossed with a beaming smile.

It was that very photo his mother now held nervously while waiting for Madam Beatriz to appear.

"Hello mother," Travis greeted his mom.

She turned to acknowledge him and purred, "Travy! You're so sweet to show up for me."

He was now twenty-two, but whenever she felt particularly emotional his mother still used his pet nickname from when he was little.

"Yes ma'am, you know I can't deny you."

She smiled sweetly, knowing that was indeed all too true.

"There's something in the air, my sweet boy. This time, I swear something's going to reveal itself to us. Some clue … some little nugget that will help lead us to Marcel."

Travis forced a smile as he did every year when she uttered these similar words of hope.

"Let's hope so!" he replied, mustering as much false enthusiasm as he could. I mean, really, if he could stop this fruitless pursuit over his long-lost great uncle's whereabouts, he'd be ecstatic.

Just then the beaded curtain rustled, and Madam Beatriz glided into the room. God, she certainly enjoyed playing the role: full skirts, gaudy jewels, and heavy theatrical eye makeup. Her hair was dyed black—although it was clear she needed to visit the hairdresser, as slight wisps of gray were beginning to show at the roots. Her hair was heavily braided, the length hanging just above the small of her back. She wore a metallic gold headband marked in the center with a blood-red crescent moon. On either side were silver stars, larger near the moon and gradually shrinking in size. *OMG*, Travis thought, *it's like she thinks she's Spiritualist Wonder Woman.*

"Eugenia—*dear!*" Madam Beatriz beamed at his mother, grasping her hand, and embracing her warmly. "It's so lovely to see you again." She turned to Travis with less enthusiasm. "Ah … I see your lovely offspring has joined us again."

"Hello, Beatriz," Travis said.

His mother winced. "Please Travy, its *Madam* Beatriz and you well know that." Eugenia turned to the spiritualist and pursed her ruby red lips, "My apologies, Madam. He was raised better."

Save me, Travis pleaded in silence.

"Well," Madam said, turning to the séance table encircled with three small stools, "let's have a seat, shall we?" A weighty crystal ball on a pedestal sat in the center of the table framed by five small lit candles. "I see you brought the photo."

"Of course," his mother replied. She sat the picture on the table, which Madam Beatriz retrieved and placed on a small easel, prominently featured in the tableau before them.

"*Spirit time! Spirit time!*" Travis nearly jumped out of his skin at the squeaky outburst.

"Matisse," Beatriz exclaimed, "please, do pipe down! We're attempting to establish a connection with the other side, and I *must* concentrate."

Madam Beatriz's African gray parrot eyed them from his perch near the front window, hopping back and forth and flapping his wings. "*Let's go! Let's go!*"

The spiritualist clapped her hands, and the lights in the room dimmed, causing the circle of candles to reflect shadows on the crystal ball. "Now, let's see if we can converse with your dear uncle this fine day." Beatriz bowed her head and began slowly passing her hands over the ball in gentle circles. Then, she raised her eyes, looking upward, and began summoning:

"We shall see what we shall see … we shall feel what we shall feel … we shall hear what we shall hear … May this day—Marcel be near!"

His mother shifted nervously next to him. As she was wont to do, she reached toward her son for a reassuring hand. Travis gently squeezed it.

This is when nothing happens, Travis thought. *Every time. And we all sit awkwardly until mother can't take it anymore and breaks the silence with a heavy emotional sigh.*

Except this time.

One of the candles surrounding the crystal ball flickered out. Once it went out and the one next to it did as well, the candle that was previously lit ignited again, glowing brighter than it had before. And, although it was a balmy New Orleans afternoon there was now a definite chill in the room.

The hair on the back of Travis's neck stood up, and his heart started beating a little faster.

Beatriz's eyes grew wide. She was looking across the table past both of them, as if she saw something—or someone—in the room. "Ooohh," she moaned. Then, she jerked spasmodically, quickly dropped her head, but jolted it right back up staring straight ahead as if in a trance.

"*Something has happened!*" Beatriz was speaking but it was not her voice. It was a male voice with an effeminate inflection. "*The spell has been awakened, and so have I. Where am I? How did I get here? I need to get out—OUT!*"

His mother jumped up off her stool. "Marcel! Is that you? We've been trying to find you ... Help us find you!" She gripped the edge of the table so fiercely Travis feared she was going to pop at least one or two of her acrylics clean off.

Matisse started squawking and flapping his wings wildly from his corner. "*Find the pendant! Find Marcel! Find the pendant! Find Marcel!*" When the parrot finished his chant, Madam Beatriz crumpled to the floor.

TEN

A DRAG DISCOVERY

 Michael rolled over in his bed in the hotel room, still struggling to wake up. What was that noise? It was knocking. "Housekeeping!"

"No flipping way!" He reached over and grabbed his phone from the nightstand. 9:38 a.m.—*no flipping way.*

He quickly hopped out of bed and ran over to the hotel room door. "Uhh ... I'm okay right now, thanks!"

"Okay," the faceless voice from the other side of the door replied. Then he heard the cart roll down the hall and a knock on the door next to his as the maid continued her rounds.

This didn't even seem possible. Michael *never* slept this late. By this time, he would have normally been up, eaten a light breakfast, headed to the gym to workout, returned for a shower, and then worked on a Fandom post. Thank God he didn't have to go to the Con today.

He was still reeling from the miraculous thing that had happened to him at the Stonewall Inn. When the pendant had reappeared in his hand, he'd gently placed it on the nightstand. It was clear the jewelry piece had something to do with his newfound abilities, but that was all he knew. He'd spent the next several hours lying awake in bed. When he'd finally fallen asleep, he'd tossed and turned all night. He'd woken up the next morning at 7:00, feeling exhausted. His mind had been flooded with unanswered questions, and he had no idea where to begin to glean any answers.

And sadly, that entire day had consisted of a full schedule at the Con. He'd forced himself through every hour, doing his best to be engaged and connected to what was going on around him. People at the convention were buzzing about the damage at the Stonewall Inn and the unbelievable news that not a single person had been injured in the explosion. He'd heard the undercurrent of comments but had shoved them to the back of his mind. If he'd thought about it, he wouldn't have made it through this day. He'd felt as if he was in a fog, going through the motions with the goal to wrap things up so he could turn his focus to the mystery of the pendant.

Then, when he'd returned to the hotel after his final commitment last night, he'd wanted to launch into looking online to see what had been released about the Stonewall incident. But he'd had two Skype calls scheduled with Fandom supporters, something he usually wouldn't do when he was out of town. However, it had been his fault—he'd can-celed the two calls when he started running out of time preparing for the New York trip—and couldn't cancel a second time. Again, he'd done his best to be "on" during the calls, but he'd been distracted.

When he'd finally finished the calls, he'd stripped off his clothes, and crawled under the covers into bed.

All that had happened took more of a toll on him than he realized, and he'd passed out after just a few minutes.

And now it was nearly 10:00 a.m.! *Holy crap.*

Well, today one way or the other he was going to get some answers.

First, food—he was starving. He pulled on his black jeans and a T-shirt. He slipped into his sneakers and shoved a ball cap over his bed-head hair. Phone in hand, he grabbed the pendant from the nightstand, secured it in his pocket, and then headed down to the hotel restaurant.

The hostess seated him at a booth in the corner near a window. He would normally be taking in the hustle and bustle of the city, but his mind was focused elsewhere.

Once he ordered breakfast, he opened his phone and did a search for Stonewall Inn, and then started scrolling through the feed. There were plenty of entries with accounts of the explosion. After reading a couple of them, he experienced a feeling of elation. Thanks to him, those people were alive. He was a hero!

But then he started reading about the Inn and the damage wrought by the boiler exploding at the restaurant next door. The Stonewall was in shambles, and there was speculation that they might not be able to rebuild. With the significance the Inn had played in the Gay Rights Movement that would be a true injustice.

As he came to the end of the latest entry, there was a news report video from one of the local TV stations. He clicked on it. The reporter stood across the street from the Inn, very close to where Michael had deposited the other Mike and the rest of the patrons he'd rescued. The reporter wrapped up his segment, saying:

"As the LGBTQ community struggles to come up with a plan to res-urrect the Inn, many long-time patrons and previous employees are arranging to meet tonight at the Hangar Bar, not far from the dam-aged establishment. With the storied history of the Stonewall Inn, there will no doubt be a concerted effort to bring it back to life."

When the video concluded, Michael read the last of the article, finished his breakfast, and returned to his room. As exhausted as he had been, reading the news accounts had released a torrent of nervous energy within him. *Best to put this to good use, I guess,* he thought, and changed into workout clothes and headed to the fitness center on the 18th floor.

He dove into his workout, trying to decide his first move to figure out what had given him his newfound abilities and very own hero identity and costume. (What *was* his hero identity going to be? What powers did he possess? Why couldn't he activate the superspeed again?) The more he pondered, the more questions flooded his mind.

Before he knew it, the ninety minutes usually allotted for his workout had flown by. He hopped off the recumbent bike and headed down to his room. Once he'd taken a shower, his head felt clearer.

Michael grabbed his laptop and worked on the day's Fandom post. With that out of the way, he returned to an online search about the incident. One of the first articles to pop up was from the *Gay City News*. It was more of a human-interest piece about the Inn's significance and a recounting of the Stonewall Riot that marked the official start of the Gay Rights Movement.

Michael absentmindedly reached for an orange from the gift basket Ned had sent and peeled it as he continued to read. He pulled a wedge off and his eyes widened at what appeared on the screen. He stared at the photo before him. The caption below read:

A core group of the patrons and employees present at the Stonewall Inn the night of the riot, later given the moniker "The Pride Pack." Standing (left to right): Bar manager Benny Sampson, bartender Tony Lewis, employees Bernardo Hernandez and Theo Main, long-time couple Jake Smith and Jeremy Janks. Seated (left to right):

Daphne Delighta (aka Tom Stamps), Stonewall matriarch Glo Bevins, Melodie Monnaie (aka Marcel DuPris), and Bambi Bendova (aka Silas Tremaine).

Melodie Monnaie—one of the drag queens in the photo sat smiling, her legs crossed, decked out in a smart bright blue sequin dress, and chunky silver heels ... and *a choker with a pendant.*

Michael retrieved his jeans from the floor and pulled the pendant from the pocket. He held it up to the photo on his laptop screen. The pendant that Melodie Monnaie wore was the *exact* pendant in his hand. She had been wearing it the night of the riot.

And now he had it.

Might someone at the gathering at Hangar Bar have information about Melodie/Marcel? Someone that would know more about the history of the Stonewall Inn. Perhaps that would put him on the path to getting answers to the questions plaguing him. Only one way to find out! He looked up the address for Hangar Bar.

It was a start.

ELEVEN

A PECK AND A SCRATCH ... CURSES!

When Madam Beatriz passed out onto the floor, Travis's mother let out a scream and also nearly fainted. The excitement of the séance and the fact that this time something had indeed happened was almost more than she could bear. Fortunately, she managed to steel herself and calm her nerves enough to direct her son to go to the aid of the spiritualist.

Travis, however, was already in action. He ran over to one of the upholstered chairs and grabbed a decorative pillow. He gathered Beatriz up, turned her over on her back, and propped up her head with the pillow.

Seeing his owner in a crumpled heap had upset the parrot, and he was flapping about and screaming all kinds of nonsense. "Will you pipe DOWN, you friggin' bird!" Travis yelled.

His mother had picked up one of the fans Madam used when feeling overheated and started fanning her. Travis slapped her cheeks lightly a couple of times. "Can you hear me? It's me, Travis—and Mrs. Beauvais." After a moment, Madam Beatriz's eyelids fluttered open. She looked dazed and out of sorts.

Eugenia walked over to a small cabinet and opened the door, revealing a snifter of brandy hidden inside.

"Mother, how did you know that was there?" Travis asked.

"Never mind," his mother replied taking the bottle and filling a small glass with a generous pour. "Give this to her."

Travis took it and lifted Beatriz's head, putting the glass to her lips. She tentatively took a sip, and then seemed to return to the same plane they were on. She took the glass from Travis and gulped a bigger swallow. Color returned to her cheeks, and she sat up.

"Well," she whispered, "I think today was a turning point—for all of us."

Travis wasn't exactly sure what she meant by that, but nevertheless nodded in agreement.

"*What now? What now?*" Matisse squawked from his perch. Madam Beatriz glanced over at her pet, and with a slight nod beckoned the bird to her side.

"Ah … my lovely friend Matisse." She reached over to pat him on the head, and then whispered, "Do your job, my pet. The time has finally arrived."

Travis didn't exactly hear what Beatriz was cooing to the parrot and didn't much care. It was time to finish things up here. He took the glass from the spiritualist and turned to set it on the séance table. As he did, Matisse flew up to the table and swiped his claw at Travis's hand, drawing a thin line of blood from the scratch he'd inflicted.

"Hey!" Travis cried, "what the hell is wrong with you?" As he started to swat the bird away, in turn Matisse gave his hand a firm peck.

"My goodness!" his mother cried out.

"Matisse, be a good boy and go back to your perch," Beatriz ordered. She turned to Travis, with a satisfied smirk. "I'm sorry about that. He's not used to seeing me in this state, and it's no doubt rattled him."

Travis had grabbed a napkin from the refreshment table and was blotting at the scratch on his hand. "I hope you're feeling well enough for us to be on our way, because I've had quite enough for one day," he said.

"Oh yes, I'll be fine. I'm *so* much better ... than I've ever been, really."

Travis gave her a sideways look in response to the cryptic comment that didn't make any sense. He turned to his mother. "Mother, I'll see you Saturday."

"Of course, dear, thank you for coming." Eugenia gave him a hug and a kiss and walked him to the door.

Lord, what a day, he thought. He looked back inside the shop to see his mother and Madam Beatriz seated again, most likely recounting the unexpected results of the séance. He noted that both of them were now partaking of the brandy.

Shaking his head, he started down the street. If there was ever a time he truly deserved beignets at Café du Monde, this was it.

Madam Beatriz spent another twenty minutes with Eugenia before sending her on her way. As she shut the shop door and flipped the sign on it from *Open* to *Closed*, she sighed and started laughing gleefully. "Well, Matisse, the day has finally arrived!" She walked over and gave her parrot a loving pat. "Now that Eugenia's uncle has finally reached out from the beyond, we can at long last activate our quest."

She retreated to her bedroom in the back of the shop and opened the drawer to her nightstand. The witch pulled out a very old book of spells titled *JewelTome*. Soon, she would complete the task passed down to her. She would find the garnet her ancestor Septima had cast the spell on centuries before and reverse it. Up till now, just a very small bit of the garnet's mystic power had been passed through her bloodline. Now it was finally time to reclaim the gem's power in its entirety.

And Eugenia's dullard of a son was going to be her unwitting accomplice.

TWELVE
ANOTHER DRAG
DISCOVERY

When Michael arrived at Hangar Bar, it felt like a neighborhood establishment that had been there forever. In fact, it had been around for twenty-five years, just a couple blocks down from the Stonewall on Christopher Street. Once his eyes adjusted to the dimly lit space, he spied a small gathering in the back near the pool table. He headed to the bar, grabbed a drink, and then made his way to the group.

As he got closer, he noticed a small sign that read: *Project Phoenix—Let's Raise the Stonewall from the Ashes!*

Nice theme, he thought. *As long as it doesn't go down the path of Dark Phoenix from the X-Men, they'll be on the right track.*

He saw someone headed his way and realized just before he reached him that it was Jason, the manager of the Stonewall. "Michael!" he said warmly, "it's good to see you in one piece. We did our best to account for everyone that was at the Inn the other night, but you were nowhere to be found. I was a bit worried."

"Hey," Michael replied, "sorry about that. The night was so unhinged—for obvious reasons. I was rattled and just grabbed my stuff and headed back to the hotel. It's awful what happened. I thought I'd come down to see if I might be able to help somehow, or at least offer moral support." *That was a lot that just came tumbling out of my mouth*, he thought.

But it appeared that Jason accepted his explanation and was just happy he had come. "Here, let me introduce you to a couple of folks," he offered.

Meeting some of the patrons might be helpful for his sleuthing, so he happily accepted the offer.

After about half an hour, Michael had met a fair number of people connected to the Stonewall Inn, either as regulars, or current or former employees. Alas, no one that seemed to be a good candidate to help him learn more about Melodie Monnaie and the pendant now secreted in his backpack.

He sat down at a table just vacated and pulled out his phone. He looked up his flight info. He was supposed to fly home the day after tomorrow. He fervently hoped by the time he got on that plane he'd at least have an inkling of what had transpired, and how the pendant had played a part.

Just then there was a smattering of applause near the front of the bar. Michael craned his neck to look at who garnered this type of welcome. There was a short, elderly man slowly walking with the aid of a cane toward the Stonewall group. Every person he passed said hello ... how amazing to see him ... what an unexpected treat, and so on. He was clearly someone that everyone knew.

As he neared the group, Jason walked over and gave the old man a gentle embrace. "It's so very good to see you, you dear man."

The old man responded, "Eh, how could I not be here? It's just too much for me to bear, knowing that the Inn has suffered so. I had to come. My spirit would not allow otherwise."

"Here, let's find you a place to sit." Jason glanced around briefly, his eyes landing on the Canadian's table. "Michael, I hope you'll allow this dear friend of mine to join you at his table?"

"Uh … sure, of course." Michael grinned, got up, and pulled out the chair next to his, offering it with a flourish. "Please, be my guest."

The old man's cheeks pinked up. "Oh my … what a delicious young man. This is an unexpected fringe benefit of venturing out tonight." He settled into the chair and put his cane under the table. "And who might you be, darlin'?"

Michael looked hard at the man. He felt familiar somehow, but he couldn't figure out why. "I'm Michael Hamm. I'm visiting from Canada. I was at the Inn on the night of the explosion."

"Ah," the old man's eyes welled with tears, "the Inn is a very important place to me, as it is to so many."

Jason walked over to the table and deposited a vodka tonic in front of the elderly guest and said, "Here you go sweetie, just how you like it." Then he turned to Michael and said, "Have you and Silas been getting acquainted?"

Silas … *Silas? My God.* Michael finally connected the vague recognition he'd had. This was Silas Tremaine … Bambi Bendova of the Pride Pack. He had been there the night of the riot, so he most certainly must know Melodie Monnaie.

"Wow!" Michael gave Silas a renewed appreciative glance. "You're part of history!"

Silas batted his eyes at the cosplayer and replied, "Why, do you mean little ol' me?"

Noting the mischievous glint in Silas's eyes, he decided to play along. "Well, I did note that you weren't exactly a tall drink of water. You must be no taller than me. Or did no one notice that when you were … Bendova, Bambi?"

Silas laughed out loud, which was then choked off by a raspy cough. "Oh my … don't do that to me, you little tart. You'll put me on the floor in no time."

Hmm …" Michael teased, "already propositioning me, I see."

"You and I are going to get along *juuust* fine," Silas returned.

Jason watched this interaction between Silas and Michael with amusement, then said, "If you want to know something about the Stone-wall and its history, there's no better source." Seeing that Silas was in good hands, Jason moved on to continue networking and developing plans to revive his bar.

Michael pulled his chair closer to Silas. "I am hoping you can help me with something. I wasn't sure I'd find someone here tonight that could, so I'm really glad I met you."

Silas took a swig of his drink. "You're cute and you're attentive. I'm all ears, dear."

THIRTEEN

INFECTED WITH
PURPOSE

Travis checked the time on his phone when he woke up. "Ugh," he moaned. It had been a week since he'd been to Madam Beatriz's with his mother. The scratch that Matisse had inflicted seemed to be getting worse, which was really pissing him off. Instead of a normal-looking scabbed wound trying to heal, his injury had an almost ebony look to it. He got up and sat in the comfy chair he had near his bedroom window. Slade, his boyfriend, had sent him a text an hour earlier: *How you feeling, hon?* The message was followed by a laughing emoji, followed up by a devil emoji.

"Bastard," Travis smiled ruefully. His head was throbbing, thanks to the late night and alcohol from the night before when he and Slade were clubbing. Even though his beau was three years older than him, he could run circles around Travis in the partying department—maddening.

And this damn wound! He realized he was scratching at it as he contemplated a barb to text to Slade in return. *That's it,* he decided. *I'm going to go down to that witch's shop and get that bird and take it to a vet to see if it's got any diseases.*

50

He dragged himself out of bed, swallowed some ibuprofen, and hopped in the shower. Then he got dressed, headed to the kitchen to grab a banana and some yogurt, and made his way to Beatriz's shop on Bienville Street.

It was 9:30 Sunday morning—way too early for there to be much activity in the French Quarter. And certainly, too early for Madam's shop to be open but he could care less. When he arrived, he rang the bell. After about fifteen seconds seeing no light come on or movement inside, he rang it again—and again. He stood outside for another minute or so. He thought it would be entirely out of character for Beatriz to be out and about this early on a Sunday morning. She sure the hell wasn't at church.

He was about to resort to banging on the door when he noted the beaded curtain parting and Madam coming toward the front of the shop in a turquoise robe. Her hair was a bit of a mess, and her face looked quite different than it had with full theatrical makeup last week.

She unlocked the door and greeted Travis with a grim smile. "Why Travis, what an unexpected ... well, not pleasure exactly—but unexpected. I wasn't anticipating your arrival until tomorrow."

Great, he thought, *another cryptic comment.* Ignoring her response, he pushed his way past Madam Beatriz into the shop.

"Well of course, please *do* come in," she said irritably and shut the door. "What brings you here on a lovely Sunday morning?"

"Your damn bird." He shoved his hand toward Beatriz. "Look at this!" he cried. "It's been a week and this fricking wound is definitely not healing. I want to take that feathered rat to a vet and get it tested. It's clearly infected me with some nastiness, and I'm going to find out what so I can get this treated."

Madam turned and walked over to the cabinet where his mother had retrieved the brandy the last time. She was chuckling and murmuring under her breath. What, Travis couldn't make out. But her odd behavior was making him all the more annoyed.

"Silly boy," she purred, "it might be that Matisse infected you with something, but there's no need for vets—or *theatrics*." She pulled a small black velvet bag from inside the cabinet and motioned for him to have a seat. He reluctantly sat down at the séance table and waited.

Beatriz opened the velvet bag and removed a small vial. "This," she said, "will help take care of that horrible scratch quite nicely."

"You're one weird broad. Why on earth didn't you give this to me when we were here?"

"Well, the timing just wouldn't have been right. But now," she smiled darkly, "turns out to be the *absolute perfect* time. Give me your hand," she instructed.

Travis reluctantly placed his hand in hers. She removed the stopper from the vial and placed three amber-colored drops of liquid across the scratch on his hand. Then, she pulled a silver ring from the bag and placed it on his right middle finger.

"Uh ... I'm not here for jewelry. Let's focus on the scratch, please."

"Oh, the ring will help—trust me," she replied.

God, get me outta this nuthouse, Travis thought.

Beatriz used a piece of gauze to massage the liquid into his wound, uttering some nonsense he couldn't understand. When she finished, the ebony wound started *moving*. It slowly snaked up from the back of his hand to his middle finger to the ring Madam Beatriz had slid on him. He watched as the ebony slithered around the center of the ring, as if there was a circle of onyx embedded in it.

The wound was gone.

But before Travis had the chance to say anything, Beatriz looked him straight in the eyes and breathed the magic word designed to enact the retrieval spell for the garnet—"*Dairym*"—*Myriad* in reverse.

Suddenly, he couldn't move a muscle and there was a buzzing sound in his ears. Then, he heard Beatriz's voice inside his head, "Now ... you have an important part to play in a very important mission. Now that your great uncle has finally broken through from where ever he is, you are going to help me find him—and more importantly, the garnet that my ancestor enchanted so many years ago. She botched that spell and it's held my family, and now me, back from gaining the fame, fortune, and full reign over dark magic that is rightfully mine." She stood and helped Travis to his feet. "You'll not remember this little revelation. But when the time is right, you'll hear my voice again. And you'll do as I ask when I ask. Until then ... *Dairym-Dairym.*"

The buzzing in his ears ceased and he realized he was now standing with Beatriz. "How ...?" he started, but Madam interrupted with a wave of her hand.

"The cure takes a toll on the body. You may have experienced a brief lapse in memory just now. Don't worry, it won't last."

"*You're ready now! You're ready now!*" Matisse squawked and flapped his wings as he hopped from right to left on his perch.

Travis shot the parrot a withering look. "You stay away from me you foul thing. Come near me again and I'll break your neck."

The parrot screeched in reply, and so did Madam Beatriz. She escorted him to the front door. "I believe we're done—for now."

Travis looked down at his hand, now fully healed. He didn't even acknowledge the ring still on his middle finger. It felt as if it had been there for years. Feeling relieved that the wound was better, he headed to Café du Monde for the second time in a week. No reason to go home without first indulging in some fresh beignets. He texted Slade to meet him there and made his way down the street.

FOURTEEN

BROOKLYN, BAMBI & A BOMBSHELL

Michael exited the subway stop at 15th Street and Prospect Park. He crossed 15th and walked along the edge of the park on Prospect Street West until he reached 4th Street where Silas lived.

Last night, he'd been eager to delve into finding out about Melodie and her pendant. After about five minutes, though, he'd realized that Silas had more vodka and tonic than someone in their seventies could handle. But he'd still wanted a chance to talk to him before flying home.

When he'd recognized Michael's disappointment, Silas had given him a glassy-eyed look across the table and said, "Why don't you come visit me tomorrow at my place in Brooklyn? I'll make us a nice brunch and we can talk about whatever you like."

Michael had perked up. "That would be wonderful!" He'd pulled out his phone and Silas recited his number and address, then agreed on a brunch time.

Michael could feel it in his bones. Today he was going to start learning more about this pendant mystery.

He soon arrived at Silas's brownstone. It was a lovely well-kept home. Pots teeming with bright-colored flowers flanked the steps. *How pretty!* A pride flag hung in the front window to the left of the steps.

Michael knocked on the door, but barely had time to finish before Silas opened it to greet him. He was in a flowing navy velour robe and house slippers brandishing a mimosa in his hand. "Good morning!" he said, as he ushered the young Canadian inside. Michael gave Silas a quick hug and followed him to the kitchen where an open backdoor led to a small deck with a table set for two. The deck opened to a nice backyard shared between Silas and his neighbors.

"I thought we'd dine al fresco, since its warm again this morning. Far better than being cooped up inside, wouldn't you agree?"

Michael grinned and accepted the offered mimosa. "Sounds great," he replied. "Can I help with anything?"

"My, so polite … your mother raised you well. We don't find boys like you around much these days," Silas remarked.

"Well, I'm Canadian, so I guess it's kind of a prerequisite."

Silas giggled and sang out, "Oh, Canada!" He then said, "Let's go sit outside. I have a quiche in the oven that will be ready soon."

They sat down and there was a small bowl of fresh cut fruit at each of their place settings and a towel covering a basket in the center of the table with freshly baked muffins. Silas removed the towel and turned to Michael. "I made these first thing this morning—blueberry. I hope you like."

They sat enjoying the muffins and the peace and quiet. It was certainly different from the Manhattan go-a-mile-a-minute energy and quite a nice change of pace. Since he was flying home tomorrow, this was a good way to decelerate and get ready for Halifax's much quieter tempo.

They made quick work of their mimosas and Silas insisted he have another, so Michael dutifully agreed. The muffins and fruit were not only tasty, but also a good buffer against becoming too tipsy from the alcohol. Michael needed his wits about him when he started his interview.

A ding from the oven signaled that the quiche was done. "I'll be out in a jiff!" Silas rose and returned a few minutes later with a slice of spinach and mushroom quiche accompanied by a salad of spring mix with carrots and red onion topped with sunflower seeds.

"This looks yummy," Michael said. And it definitely was. While they ate, Silas shared some of his neighborhood's history and his life in New York. When they had finished, Michael insisted he clear the table and volunteered to make Silas another mimosa, which he readily agreed to. Michael filled his own glass with just orange juice this time. When he returned, he set the glasses down on the table, sat, and said, "Can we talk a little about the Stonewall and your friends back then?"

"Of course, darling," Silas returned. "It was such an amazing and tumultuous time, but I was so proud to be there for it."

Michael pulled a copy of the photo he'd printed from the online article he'd read. He showed it to Silas and said, "Tell me about that night and your drag queen friends in the pic with you."

That was all Silas needed. For the next fifteen minutes, he regaled Michael with what occurred that night and his friendships with Marcel and Tom. "The three of us were fast friends, and we did nearly everything together. After that night," she said sadly, "it was just me and Tom."

Michael sat up straighter. "Only you and Tom, but what about Marcel? What happened to him?"

Silas sighed. "We don't really know. It's a mystery that's never been solved. Marcel disappeared that night, never to be seen again."

"Holy crap," Michael responded, absorbing this information. He then reached down to his backpack beside him and unzipped the side pocket where he'd stored the pendant. "When I was at the Stonewall the night of the explosion, I found something in the corner under a floorboard just before everything went crazy. When I saw this photo online, it became clear that this—" Michael placed the pendant on the table between them, "—must have belonged to Marcel."

Silas's eyes widened and he gasped, "My God—you found this?"

"Yes," Michael replied, "and I feel like there's more to the pendant than meets the eye. Do you know anything about it?"

Silas's cheeks had paled, erasing the glow from the mimosas and lovely morning. After taking a significant gulp of his drink, Silas reached for the pitcher of water and poured a glass, drinking down the entire thing. The hydration seemed to help, as Silas then said, "I do know something about it."

The hair on the back of Michael's neck stood up. *Finally!* He was going to get some info about Melodie and the pendant.

Silas looked up briefly as he brought forth his memories connected to the pendant. "I remember Melodie arriving that night. She was always a confident queen, but that evening she seemed to be particularly self-assured and beaming. We were seated together in the bar before the riot—Tom was on stage. And—as usual—we were dishing instead of dutifully watching Daphne's performance." He giggled. "And the piercing glares we got from Tom periodically confirmed he was well aware of it. Anyway ... Marcel was very proud of that pendant. He'd just finished making it earlier that day. He told me that the garnet he'd used at its center had been passed down through generations of his family and ended up with him. His sister Lacey wasn't a fan of loud or gaudy jewelry and—big surprise—Marcel loved it, so she'd gladly let him have it.

It was—still is—impressive," Silas said, gently touching the pendant. "But there was more to this jeweled piece than met the eye." Then he got up and motioned for Michael to follow him inside. They went to the living room, and Michael sat down on an overstuffed sofa as Silas went to a small desk in the corner. He removed a keychain from his pocket and inserted a delicate key in the lock on the desk drawer, then opened it and pulled out a small silver sequined purse.

Michael started. "Is that ... Melodie's purse from that night?"

Silas nodded and joined Michael on the sofa. "It was the only thing that remained of Melodie after the raid. I found it underneath the pool table in the corner of the bar." He opened the purse and pulled a small, yellowed piece of paper folded into quarters. "This piece of paper has everything to do with that pendant."

Michael had brought the pendant inside with him, and it now rested between them on the sofa cushion. The sunlight streaming through the window caused the stone to seemingly glow from within.

"Melodie told me that he'd spoken these words," Silas held out the piece of paper, "to enchant the pendant. It is a copy of the spell that had been cast over the garnet more than a century before when one of his ancestors visited a Creole witch in a bayou outside of New Orleans. The spell, he said, was to protect its wearer."

Silas offered the paper to Michael, who unfolded it and read the message inside. It consisted of a phrase in French, with an English translation scribbled underneath. He folded it up, trying to absorb all Silas had shared. "So, do you think the spell worked?"

Silas replied, "I think it did. But in a way Melodie certainly didn't expect. I think when she was in danger that night, somehow the spell took hold and worked in a way no one could ever have been able to comprehend. She may have been protected, but the end result was her vanishing, never to be seen again." Silas took the folded paper and returned it to its home in Melodie's purse, snapping it shut. He handed the purse to Michael. "Somehow, I think you are meant to have this."

"Gosh," Michael responded, "I was thinking that you should have the pendant, as you had such a strong connection with Melodie. It feels like it belongs with you."

Silas scoffed, "Nonsense ... there's a reason you were able to rediscover it all these many years later—it can't be accidental. You were destined to have the pendant, and whatever charm it holds. And it's only fitting that the paper with the spell that bestowed that power on this little jewel accompanies its new owner."

"I ... don't know what to say," Michael replied. He was still reeling from what he'd just learned about Melodie ... the pendant ... the disappearance ... and the spell.

Silas reached over and gave Michael a firm hug. "Sweetie, you coming out all this way for a visit, keeping me company, and sharing this discovery—well, what more can an old queen ask for on a Sunday morning?"

Michael returned Silas's hug. "Well, thank *you*. I certainly didn't know what to expect when I came here this morning, but this is more than I ever hoped for. I can tell from the reception you received at the Hangar Bar last night that you're revered and respected ... and you can add my respect to theirs."

"Oh you ... don't make me get all misty. You're a sweetheart."

They spent another half-hour chatting about very nearly nothing, and then Silas offered to walk Michael back to the subway station. He explained that he liked to get out of the house on Sunday afternoons to visit a nearby flower shop. Michael strolled back to the subway with him, and gave him one last hug and peck, promising to stay in touch. Silas touched Michael's cheek and wished him a safe trip home.

As he rode the train back to Manhattan, Michael pulled the slip of paper out of the purse concealed in his backpack and reread it. Somehow his discovery of the pendant the night of the explosion had revived the protective spell Marcel had cast the night of the riot. And he was now the lucky recipient of its mystic power.

God, he thought. He'd always loved New York for its energy and magic. Now he was in possession of some type of energy and magic he could never have even comprehended.

Melodie ... wherever you are ... thank you. And if there's a way to find out where you went, I'm going to figure it out.

FIFTEEN

HERO
WORSHIP

"You are such a nerd!" Travis had just arrived at Slade's apartment after work. His boyfriend wanted a date night, and now that he was feeling better, he was more than happy to oblige.

Slade ignored the tease and continued playing his video game. *Jesus,* Travis thought, *even when he's just splayed out on the couch, he is a sexy guy.* His boyfriend took great care of his body, and he had a beautiful face to match. Dirty blond hair, blue eyes, chiseled jaw, and that dimple in his chin, which always drove Travis nuts. At 6'2" and 205 pounds of lean muscle, it was hard not to pounce on Slade every time he saw him. He was a striking contrast to Travis's shorter 5'11" frame and his lightly colored Creole skin and dark hair. Travis wasn't what he would consider a looker, but Slade seemed to be infatuated with him. And that was perfectly fine with him.

Given how he'd felt the past week dealing with recovering from the nasty scratch on his hand, he knew he hadn't been the best company. Tonight he was determined to make up for that.

When he reached the end of his game, Slade got up and went over and kissed Travis—a long deep one. It took Travis's breath away. When he was finished, Travis breathed, "My that's a much better greeting than I usually get."

Slade leaned down and whispered in his ear, "Well, get ready for an adventure tonight." He gave him another deep kiss and grabbed Travis's crotch, and he immediately responded.

Just then Slade's phone pinged. "Ah, our dinner must be here," he said. "I'll be right back."

He left the apartment and returned shortly with Chinese from Travis's favorite spot.

They dished out their food, poured wine, and sat down at the dinner table and spent time just chatting and enjoying each other's company.

This is so nice, Travis thought. *He can be a bit self-absorbed some-times, but when he shows up, he does it big-time.*

When they'd finished dinner, Slade cleared the table and let Travis drink the last of his wine. Then, he pulled him up by his hand and planted another very deep kiss on his lips as he slowly led him to the couch. "Now," Slade said with a bit of a rough tone, "you're going to sit here and you're going to wait for me. And while you do, you're going to wear this." From his back pocket Slade produced a blindfold and quickly slid it over Travis's eyes.

"What the ...?" This was certainly new territory. They'd never been ones for anything even remotely kinky before. He wasn't quite sure how he felt about it. But before he could say another word, Slade gave him another deep kiss and whispered, "No peeking."

"Mmm ... well ... okay."

Satisfied, Slade retreated to the bedroom. He was in there for quite some time, and Travis was getting restless. He was tempted to slide the blindfold off and peek, but he vowed to be patient. He reminded himself of his behavior over the past week and that this was the night to make amends. And, let's face it—he was putty when it came to his boyfriend.

After a few more minutes, he heard Slade emerge from the bedroom. There was an odd rustling noise as he walked that mystified Travis. What was he up to?

He didn't have to wait long to find out. He could feel Slade standing in front of him and, before he knew it, he felt Slade's lips on his again as he slowly slid off the blindfold. It was another long deep ardent kiss, and truthfully it and the wine were making him feel a bit lightheaded.

When they finished kissing, he opened his eyes and stared at his boyfriend. He was standing before him fully costumed as Batman. It was clear he'd had this custom-made, as the spandex fit his frame to a tee. He wore leather briefs and a utility belt, a cowl, tall leather boots, and a cape that fell to the middle of his calves. He'd used black makeup around his eyes to make them pop, and they were piercing.

Slade was a true nerd in every sense of the word. He was a gamer, an ardent comic book reader, couldn't wait for the release of the next superhero blockbuster, and always wanted to do some slutty version of a superhero when they hit the French Quarter on Halloween. None of it was really Travis's thing, but he gladly tolerated it, as Slade was so terrific to him. This, however, was another level altogether. And, he had to admit, his boyfriend was a hot-as-hell hero.

"Wow …" was all he could think to say.

"Well … what do you think—pretty cool huh?" Slade was grinning from ear to pointy ear. He was very pleased with the work he'd put into the dinner, the costume—all of it.

"Holy hot shit, Batman," Travis teased, "I will say you've taken me completely by surprise. I think I actually like it."

"Oh, you'll like it," Slade said mischievously. He reached out a gloved hand, pulled Travis up, and wrapped the cape around him. Travis realized the cape must have made the rustling sound when Slade came back into the living room. "Get ready for some hero worship, baby."

"You are such a nerd." Travis's heart was racing, and his dick was throbbing. He willingly followed Slade to the bedroom.

Travis woke up and rolled over in bed, reaching out for Slade to snuggle. But all he felt was a bundle of cape. He sighed; Slade was always the early riser. He wished Slade had roused him when he woke up. It would have been nice to snuggle after the night they'd just had. He smiled thinking about all they'd done, and how Slade's little Batman role-play had amped things up. He might have to rethink this whole nerdy business.

Travis covered himself with the cape and lay there for a few more minutes before getting up. He showered, dressed, and went out into the kitchen of Slade's apartment. He found a note on the table that his beau had left: *Coffee in the pot, headed to Charmaine's for pastries—back in a bit.* He'd signed it with his usual "*S*" with a slash through it and a heart.

He sighed, "I'm so lucky." He poured some coffee and checked his phone—nothing that interesting. He glanced up from his cell and noticed that Slade's laptop was open to a webpage. He pulled it toward him and looked at the screen. Some site called Fandom was open, and it appeared that Slade had been perusing some guy on it named Michael Hamm.

Hmm ...what the hell is this? Travis thought as he studied the guy's photos in various superhero costumes at the top of his page. Before he had a chance to look any further, something strange happened. The ring that Madam Beatriz had slid on his finger started to glow. He suddenly heard the buzzing in his ear he'd heard the week before when he'd visited the spiritualist and again heard her voice in his mind.

"Well … this is something," he heard her voice say. "This boy … this Michael Hamm. He has something to do with the garnet we need to find. You're going to find this boy, and we're going to do whatever is necessary to get that jewel back to me. Find Michael Hamm!"

Then the buzzing ceased. Travis wasn't sure what just happened. One minute he was looking at Slade's laptop, and then the next was a blank. He shook his head vigorously. What was going on with him?

A few minutes later, Slade returned with pastries from Charmaine's. "Hey hon," he greeted Travis and gave him a quick peck on the cheek. "Sleep well?"

His attention had returned to the laptop, and as he turned it toward Slade he asked, "And exactly *who* is Michael Hamm?"

SIXTEEN

HOME TO
HALIFAX

"Who could you possibly need to text already?"

Michael's best friend Kristin had picked him up at the airport and was driving him to his apartment.

"I'm texting this very nice man I met in New York to thank him for his hospitality and for being so helpful. I promised to let him know when I arrived home."

"Ooohhh," she teased, "Mikey made a love connection in the Big Apple."

"*Veerry* funny. As if! No, this is a kindly old man named Silas. I met him when I went to the Hangar Bar after the Stonewall exploded. We kind of hit it off and had more in common than I ever dreamed. He had me over to his house for brunch yesterday."

Kristin sighed, "Of course, how dumb of me to think you'd actually have a booty call while you're in New York! I mean, seriously, you've got to live a little. You're not getting any younger, you know." She poked him in the side playfully, knowing it would irritate him.

"Hey! Stop that! And trust me … this trip became more illuminating than any I've ever taken in my life. There was no time for tricks. And," he gave her a sideways glance, "I DO partake in the local fruit from time to time when I travel." He gave her a cheesy grin and she moaned.

"Well, not often enough in my opinion."

Kristin pulled up in front of his building and Michael grabbed his backpack and suitcase from the trunk. He promised to touch base soon to go to dinner, then waved goodbye.

When he opened the door to his apartment, his cat Grayson came slinking down the stairs. "Gray-gray!" He swept up his cat and gave him a dozen kisses until the cat had enough. He pushed his way out of Michael's arms and sauntered over to the kitchen for a snack.

He lugged his suitcase upstairs and plopped down on his bed. The New York trip had been good for him. It had gotten him slightly back in the swing of things. The discovery of the pendant and the resulting effects though had taken a toll on his energy level. He was grateful to be home to unwind and recharge, and for his normal routine to help him feel centered again.

He lay there for a few minutes enjoying the cozy feel of his bed. Then he noted his stomach was grumbling. I guess Grayson wasn't the only one who needed food. He headed downstairs to scrounge up something to eat. While he was snacking at the kitchen table, his roommate Beth walked through the front door, groceries in hand.

"Hey," she said, "welcome back."

"Hey back at you … Oh good, I see you've brought me food." Michael gave her a sickeningly sweet yearning expression.

"Back off bitch—don't make me cut you the minute I see you after a week."

"Well, I can tell you missed me." He got up from the table and gave her a hug, then helped her unpack and put the groceries away.

"How was it?" Beth asked.

"Well," Michael started, "unlike any trip I've ever had to New York. You know … tight costumes, endless fans … a near-death experience … a rebirth … the usual."

"I see you're as weird as ever. What do you mean a *near-death experience?*"

Michael wasn't surprised she hadn't heard what happened at the Stonewall Inn. They sat down in the living room, and he proceeded to tell her about his trip and the explosion.

"Holy shit! It's a good thing you're okay. Your half of the rent is due in a week."

He laughed. "Well, oh friend of mine, thanks for your concern. It's *sooo* good to be home."

"And … what's the rebirth remark about?"

Michael considered telling Beth about what had *really* happened during the trip. But he stopped short. He wasn't exactly a superhero (or was he?), but he knew all too well how sharing this kind of secret with close friends and loved ones turned out for his comic book heroes. He needed to figure out this hero/pendant stuff more thoroughly and gain some confidence with it before even considering letting someone else in on the secret. "Let's just say I discovered things about myself that were buried until now. I've got some inner work to do."

"Uhh … cryptic." Beth looked at him cynically. "Let me know when you figure out who you are."

They hung out for another forty-five minutes. Then it was time for him to head upstairs, check his Fandom page, do some social media posts, and hit the hay.

A week passed. The cosplayer returned to his normal day-to-day activities: daily gym visits, creating content, and working on a few new costumes. He also reached out to San Diego Comic-Con. He was working on his schedule and commitments for the convention. It was hard to believe it was just a few weeks away.

On Saturday morning, he woke up early and got ready for a day full of Skype calls with Fandom supporters. This was always a mixed bag. He knew some of his followers were not the best on the calls, as they were often nervous speaking with him.

Funnily enough, he was usually nerve wracked nearly every time he got ready for a call. Something about the chats was almost like making a mini-personal appearance, and he felt he needed to be "on." He believed it was up to him to ensure things continued along so neither side suffered awkward silences.

A few of his supporters were quite fun to talk with and brought an endless array of topics and questions to their chats, which made it a lot easier for him, and those he looked forward to.

He flipped open his laptop and took a look at his schedule. *Hmm… Tommy, Chris… those are usually good calls.* He scrolled further down and groaned, *Oh man, Slade Bishop.*

Slade was an interesting character. In the six months since he'd joined Michael's Fandom, it had become clear that Slade had a sometimes uncomfortable crush on the cosplayer. Michael could usually manage to keep the conversation going, but Slade often became a little starstruck, resulting in some of their calls feeling uneven and awkward. He knew Slade also had a secret desire to do his own cosplay someday. From their chats, it was clear that Slade was quite hot and would have no problem filling out a spandex suit and looking very impressive. Sometimes he'd ask Michael endless questions about where he got his costumes, how he worked on constructing pieces, what he used for eye black, how he affixed masks, and so on. This line of questioning helped immensely to get through a call, as he had a wealth of knowledge to share and it took the attention off Michael Hamm, the cosplay crush and instead focused on Michael Hamm, the costume creator. Hopefully some of that talk would be part of today's chat and it would fly by.

Michael went about getting his room camera-chat ready, went downstairs for a bite to eat, and then hopped in the shower. Later, he sat down at his laptop, scribbling some notes about his first few callers, so he had something to fall back on topic-wise in case he needed it. Grayson pushed the door to Michael's room open and jumped onto his lap as he finished his notes. "You can't be up here in a few minutes, mister. It's marathon call day."

His cat looked up at him for an expectant petting, and Michael willingly obliged. Then he planted a couple of mushy kisses on Grayson and placed the cat on his bed. The feline dutifully curled up between two pillows where he could nap as well as keep watch on his owner. This was a well-practiced routine for the two.

The pendant sat on his desk out of view next to the laptop. He had kept it with him constantly. Until he figured out how to reactivate the power he'd been gifted with in New York, he would not let it out of his sight. He'd "practiced" a few times during the past week trying to get the pendant to respond to his uttering of the word: *"Myriad."* He'd even dressed in full costume a few times to see if that played a part in the equation to unleash the pendant's enchantment. But nothing he'd tried had worked.

Okay, let's get onstage and make the first call. Michael messaged Tommy to see if he was ready to chat, and then hit the *Call* button. Grayson waited until his master was a few minutes into the call, then wrapped his tail around his body, closed his eyes, and drifted off to sleep.

SEVENTEEN

REVELATIONS HEROIC & EVIL

 Slade was giddy. He couldn't wait for his call with Michael today to finally reveal the surprise he had in store!

Last week, when he returned to his apartment and Travis confronted him about Michael, he'd sheepishly confessed that he'd been a fan of the pro-cosplayer for quite a while. Earlier that year, Slade had decided to join Michael's Fandom page.

Travis had been unnerved by this discovery, but now that he'd found out, Slade had to admit he was relieved. He'd done his best to reassure his boyfriend that this was solely about cosplay and nothing more.

But he wasn't a dummy. Slade had known when he shared this with Travis, he'd jump to the irrational conclusion that he was competing with Michael for Slade's attention. While Slade confessed to himself that this might be partially true (he would periodically sneak away to peruse anything he could find about Michael online and get a thrill when there was a notification that he'd posted something new), Travis had his heart. Besides, what gay guy didn't have his own sexy distractions and fantasies? (Answer—pretty much all of them.)

Slade's attempt to expose Travis (in more ways than one) to his cosplay passion by revealing his newly finished Batman costume had been a success. It got his attention and Travis had admitted there was something more to it than just dressing up. Slade hadn't revealed the next part of his cosplay immersion plan to Travis yet, and he knew he had some work ahead. But his success last weekend had provided him with renewed confidence.

Slade had spent extra time at the gym that morning. He'd wanted to be pumped for the call. When he got back to his place, he'd enjoyed a good long shower and took his time suiting up as Batman. When he was in full costume, he only had to apply the eye black, don the cowl, and he'd be ready to surprise Michael.

Fifteen minutes later, he was set. He sat down where Travis had confronted him with Michael's site the week before and turned on his laptop. He opened Skype and took in how he looked on cam. He wanted to be sure everything appeared perfect. It was about three minutes before they were scheduled to start.

Just then Travis texted him. *Aagh!* Sometimes his timing sucked! Slade quickly pulled off a glove, grabbed his phone, and read: *Hey! How's your day? Have any free time in the next couple of hours? Thought we could grab lunch.*

Slade hastily texted a reply: *Sorry hon … at the gym right now and just started working out. How about dinner tonight?*

He saw the continuous "…" on his phone, indicating that Travis was responding. Then, the dots disappeared, and no reply came. Slade got an uneasy feeling. Travis knew him too well. Even when he wasn't around, he had an uncanny sense to detect when Slade was telling a fib.

Suddenly Michael popped up on Skype, "Hey Slade—ready when you are!"

At the same time the answering text came through from Travis: *Okay. See you tonight.*

God, I hope he's not on to me, Slade thought. He pulled his glove back on and turned his attention to the laptop and typed: *"So ready!"* He then waited for Michael's call. He was excited and nervous!

Travis put his phone back in his gym shorts. He was upset. As he grabbed the dumbbells to do another set of bicep curls, he looked in the mirror and pumped. When he finished the set, he cut his workout short, and headed to the locker room to shower and change.

You're not here at the gym, you bastard. And I'm going to get to the bottom of this.

Michael started to utter his usual, "Well hello! What's going on!" greeting and stopped. He was astonished to see Batman staring back at him on the screen.

"Well ... what do you think?" Slade beamed in his costume at the camera. He immediately jumped up to reveal Batman in his entirety to Michael. He couldn't resist pulling the cape up and posing and flexing.

"Uhh ... wow!" Michael was completely taken aback. This was a twist. And it was weird. He needed to make sure he didn't let on that it was uncomfortable though, so he said, "Gosh ... I guess you made it happen! Congrats!"

Slade was oblivious. He was too excited about his big reveal to Michael. He proceeded to go on about every piece of his costume, where he'd gotten them, and then told him how he had surprised his boyfriend last weekend. When he started to talk about what happened after he'd made the big reveal with Travis, Michael wanted to crawl under the table.

He was trying to figure out how to gracefully change the course of the conversation and get things back to more neutral territory. As he wracked his brain, he realized the garnet in the center of the pendant had begun to glow. *Uh-oh … what the hell is going on?* he thought. He was so distracted by the pendant he hadn't realized that Slade had stopped speaking mid-sentence. Then, he heard what he'd just *thought* moments before … but it was coming from two different voices on the other side of the camera.

Slade breathed in, "Uh-oh."

Travis had just unexpectedly arrived at his apartment. "What the hell is going on?"

Slade gave a sideways glance at Travis, and then said nervously, "Hi babe! What a nice surprise. What are you doing here?"

Travis ignored Slade's feeble greeting. "When I texted you, I was *AT* the gym. Clearly you were lying, so I cut my workout short and decided to come over and see what was so compelling that you thought lying to me was a good idea, and …" Travis felt like he'd been flung back a week as he looked at Slade's open laptop and saw Michael Hamm on cam. Now he was mad. "Oh, I SEE. You had a date with your online boyfriend. I think I need to meet him myself."

The cosplayer thought, *Oh crap. I don't know what's going on and I don't think I want to.* He looked at Slade, who was clearly dying of embarrassment. Michael whispered, "Uh … why don't I take a rain check and we can chat another time."

Just then Travis walked up behind Slade and put his face next to his boyfriend's masked one so Michael could see him. "Wait a minute there, cosplay boy. I want to know what's going on here … uhh … *ooohhh.*" Suddenly Travis's eyes glazed over.

"Aargh!" Michael screamed out in agony. When Travis appeared on cam, Michael experienced a piercing pain shooting through his brain—something that had never happened before. And it hurt like hell.

Grayson woke from his sleep and looked at the screen where Travis's face had appeared. His hair went up on end as if he was electrified; he arched his back and hissed at the laptop.

The pain was not stopping—Michael rubbed both of his temples. He'd closed his eyes tight and now felt as if there was a bright light in front of him. And there *was* a bright light—a bright red one. When he opened his eyes, the garnet was glowing brighter, and then a crimson ray shot from it and hit his mirror. When the light hit the glass, his cat hissed again and growled.

Then a voice—*from inside his room*—was yelling at him. "Michael! *Michael!* End the call! Shut the laptop *NOW!*"

With his head still throbbing, he struggled to look around his room. His eyes landed on the mirror, and he froze. The glass was entirely bathed in red—and Melodie Monnaie was looking straight at him from inside the mirror! "Michael!" Melodie said again very firmly, "SHUT THAT CALL DOWN NOW."

Michael turned to the laptop. He saw Travis wearing an evil grin. In a voice that sounded entirely different from what Michael had just heard seconds ago, Travis said, "Oh you can go, but you can't escape me now that I've found you. See you soon, hero boy."

"MICHAEL!" Melodie yelled his name again and with that Michael slammed the laptop shut.

EIGHTEEN

MELODIE IN
THE MIRROR

 When Michael shut the laptop, the searing pain in his head stopped immediately. He had closed his eyes again, as the pain had been intense and they felt incredibly sensitive to light. After about thirty seconds, he slowly opened his eyes. His vision was slightly out of focus, so he shut them again and rubbed them. This time when he reopened them, he could finally see clearly.

He stared at Grayson, who had hopped off the bed and came to sit beside him. "Gray-gray, what the hell just happened?" His cat rubbed up against his leg in response. Then, seeing that his owner was recovering, turned around, and returned to his place on the bed.

"Are you all right, dear?"

Michael yelled in surprise and jumped out of his seat. It took him a split second to realize who was speaking to him. That vision of Melodie in the mirror *wasn't a vision*. There in the glass, still bathed in the red glow that emanated from the pendant, was Melodie.

"Melodie?" he said. "Or ... Marcel ...? Or ... uh ... is that really you? How is this happening?"

"This will take a bit of time, my boy. Why don't you lie down on your bed, and I'll do my best to fill you in."

Michael obligingly walked over to his bed and plopped down. *Well,* he thought, *this is totally crazy. I may as well lie down like I'm in a therapy session.* He situated himself so he had Melodie in his view, and Grayson curled up next to him. He took a moment to survey Melodie's surroundings inside the mirror. It looked like she was still at the Stonewall. "How are you still at the Inn?" he asked.

"I'm not really, at least not anymore. But I think because it was the last place I was and have a memory of before the riot, it's the surrounding my mind conjured."

"Okay … so where *are* you, exactly?"

Melodie sat down on a barstool, crossed her legs, and took a sip of a cocktail. "That's a good question. When the spell I'd placed on the pendant saved me from the riot, it did something that I didn't expect. It literally saved me by removing me from the Inn and trapping me inside the pendant. More specifically, inside the garnet that has been in my family's possession for generations—which, I imagine, is why you see me bathed in this ruby red glow. I'm trapped like a genie in a bottle. Or, rather, like Jeannie, as in *I Dream Of.*"

The reference to the 1960s sitcom didn't register with Michael, so Melodie continued, "I've been in this—other place—ever since. Just enough of the garnet's magic remained with me and has been keeping me alive here.

Then, when you were at the Inn and discovered the pendant and reactivated the enchantment by uttering the word on the back, you were able to tap into the rest of its available power. The spell was meant to protect, and your being in a superhero costume at the time seems to have given you the unique ability to tap into its magic and actually *become* a real superhero.

Time moves a bit differently in here. The seconds when you acti-vated the spell right before the explosion and saved all those people was a much longer period for me. I have a bit of talent for creating traf-fic-stopping looks ... and let's face it, you were an excellent specimen to design a costume for. So, I used my connection to the magic to help design your superhero look. That night the word on the back of the pen-dant became more than just a way to activate the spell—it also became the name of a true-to-life superhero—*Myriad*."

"So, you designed that costume!" Michael exclaimed.

'I did," Melodie replied. "I hope you like it ... and the name of your new hero identity."

"I love it," Michael confessed. "I mean; this is like a childhood dream come true. And that costume fit me perfectly."

"Well, dear, it's formed from magic. And, let's face it, you're quite the inspiration. I had plenty of ammunition to conjure up something yummy."

Michael grinned and said sheepishly, "Gee ... thanks. So ... Myriad ..."

"I thought it the perfect name for you. It seems your powers derive from your cosplay heroes, which means you have endless possibilities to draw from when you need them. I have to say, getting to know you remotely has been an education. Who knew there would ever be a day when someone could earn a living dressing up? I was born at the wrong time!"

Michael laughed. "Myriad—I like it. But why is it that when I tried to manifest powers on my own after the explosion, I've not been successful?"

Melodie shifted uncomfortably on her barstool and took a good swig of her drink. "Well, this is where it gets interesting ... and most cer-tainly dangerous."

"Well naturally," Michael returned. "I mean, there must be a hitch somewhere—lay it on me."

Melodie replied ruefully, "There's a reason you experienced that piercing pain during the call with Slade. It was because of his boyfriend Travis—who, by the way, happens to be my great-nephew."

"What?? And he somehow has powers too?"

"Well, not exactly, at least not by choice. You see, his mother Eugenia is my niece. She's been trying to solve the mystery of my disappearance ever since she learned of it. Every year, she makes an appointment with a Madam Beatriz who works out of a dingy shop in the French Quarter in New Orleans. The psychic conducts a séance trying to contact me. When you reactivated the pendant's magic, it somehow also gave me the ability to communicate with her for the first time. And—it also brought to light that Beatriz is a descendant of the very bayou witch who cast the spell over my family's garnet."

Michael rubbed his head again. "This is a lot. You're making my head hurt with all these revelations."

"I wish that was all I have to share," Melodie returned. "Alas, it gets even worse."

"Oh great … okay. Tell you what, I'm going to get some ibuprofen, and then you can darken my day—or enlighten it—further." Michael got up from the bed and disappeared down the hall into the bathroom. When he returned, he noted that Melodie had taken advantage of the little break and refreshed her lipstick. She slipped the tube into her cleavage when she was finished. Michael had a sudden thought and went over to his closet. When he returned, he held Melodie's purse in his hands.

"Oh, you little tease!" Melodie groaned. "I forgot that my dear friend Silas passed my purse on to you. Little did he know I would actually be speaking with you!"

"God, it's weird to think you were actually *with* us when I visited him!" Michael held up the purse. "We're going to figure out how to get this back to you so you're not stashing makeup in your boobs."

"Ha! Well, we'll see if we can make that happen somehow. I've been without a purse to complete this outfit for many years. It's drag-gone embarrassing."

Now it was Michael's turn to groan. "Uh ... not sure what your day job is ... or was ... but hang on to it. So ... you said there's more?"

Melodie's cheery demeanor evaporated. "Yes, there's more." She stood and began pacing. "Beatriz has been trying to track down my family's garnet for years. You see, her descendant didn't exactly do what she'd intended. The spell was not supposed to provide protection and prosperity to our family. It was actually meant to *siphon* anything we might enjoy and transfer it to the bayou witch. My ancestors who'd traveled to America did so with considerable wealth they'd amassed overseas. The witch knew this prior to Marie—my relative who visited her—arriving with the garnet to enchant. When Septima—the witch—succeeded in casting the siphoning spell six times, it was supposed to grant her and her descendants immeasurable dark magic, power, and wealth. She botched Marie's curse, but Septima succeeded in casting the siphoning spell correctly three times before her death. When she died, her daughter Gabrielle tried to pick up where her mother had left off. But her daughter wasn't as gifted in witchcraft as her mother, and she never succeeded in casting a single successful siphoning spell.

Meanwhile, my family was enjoying even greater prosperity in America. As time wore on, their wealth and power continued to grow. My grandfather Benjamin was a shrewd businessman who made some very smart investments in oil and rail. Our family became well established in New Orleans with a large estate, which had been a former plantation outside the city."

Michael was absorbing the story and taking it all in. He could see Melodie was growing weary from recounting everything to someone for the first time. He thought she could use a break, so the cosplayer teased, "Ah! So, the moral of the story is: if I can rescue you from the pendant, you'll be rich, and I'll have a sugar daddy. Or … sugar mama."

Melodie let out a huge laugh. "Hardly, my dear hero boy. Do you think my family was thrilled when they discovered I was not only gay but also a drag queen? No, Michael, I was cut off from my family's money years before I finally fled New Orleans and headed to New York City. I'm afraid you'll still have to sing—or cosplay—for your supper."

"Ah well … worth a shot! So," Michael continued, "ultimately the story must come to Beatriz's family being on the brink of succeeding in gaining great power and wealth by stealing the garnet and correcting the original siphoning spell."

Melodie stared at him. "Well, way to cut a drag queen's soliloquy short! But yes, you're right. And she intends to use Travis as her brain-washed pawn to do it, since he's a relative of Marie, the one who started this with her visit to Septima over a hundred years ago."

"I still don't understand how I managed to reactivate the power of the pendant. And why it doesn't work when I try to bring forth Myriad on my own."

"Ah," Melodie replied, "well … that's kind of the big reveal. Since the garnet's power isn't yet yours to command in its entirety, it appears you'll only be able to bring forth the pendant's magic when there's a need for a hero. Let me get another drink and I'll …"

Michael sat up on the bed when Melodie's voice started to fade. In another few seconds, the ruby red surrounding the drag queen began to glow brightly and then a flash of crimson bolted from the mirror back to the pendant. Michael's glass was empty, and Melodie had disappeared back inside the garnet again.

"Crap!" he cried out. He'd been getting such valuable information and there was still more of the story to be unearthed. He absentmind-edly grabbed Grayson and rested him on his lap. He stroked the feline's back for a few minutes, thinking about everything he'd just learned over the past half-hour. "Well Gray-Gray, I seem to be having this thought an awful lot lately." He looked down at his cat and said, "Now what?"

Then he groaned, *Oh man … I know "now what," at least right now. Another Skype call. This one had better be a helluva lot less sinister!* He sat Grayson back on the bed, walked over to his desk, and opened his laptop again.

"My life is getting freaking weird."

NINETEEN

PLANNING A
HERO'S DEMISE

Beatriz was ebullient. When Travis connected with Michael on Slade's call, she'd been immediately alerted and possessed Travis. This confirmed that Michael now had the garnet. Hoping she was powerful enough to use the online connection, she had started casting the siphoning spell the minute she overtook Travis's body. But she hadn't expected or anticipated that Marcel—or his alter ego Melodie—would intervene from the beyond. And, when the drag queen succeeded in getting the cosplayer to abruptly end the call, her chance of emerging victorious had been dashed.

Well. She may not have been successful *this* time but at least now she knew who had the pendant. She just had to figure out how to get Travis close enough to Michael to seize the garnet and achieve her ultimate goal.

"*Power soon! Power soon!*" Matisse called out from his perch.

"Quite right, my little pet," Beatriz mused. "Hmm … I'm going to have to do a little online research about this Michael Hamm."

The witch made a pot of strong coffee, adding a little brandy to give it a kick. She entered: *Michael Hamm cosplay*—into the search field on her computer and up popped several images and links to various tidbits on him. After about ten minutes, Beatriz discovered Michael lived in Halifax, had been doing cosplay for a number of years, and made a recent appearance in New York.

Then she came across his Fandom page. "Ah ... what's this?" She clicked the link and read the brief description of the perks of joining the cosplayer's Fandom page, including a monthly Skype chat. This must have been what led to that fool Slade's Batman costume and online call with Michael earlier. "Good heavens Matisse," she said, "the things people do to make a living today while I'm sitting here barely getting by! Well, I'm on the verge of success; I can feel it in my bones. I'm one spell away from being powerful and rich!"

She continued perusing the web, scrolling and studying the entries that came up. There was a recap of the New York Comic-Con and Michael was mentioned. She clicked on the link and read:

Michael made New York his first Con appearance after the pandemic. "The past couple of years our lives changed a lot, he shared. "But I have to say this trip to the New York Con has been a trip like no other."

The post concluded noting that Michael's next appearance would be at the mother of all nerdy gatherings, the San Diego Comic-Con.

"Ah," Beatriz exclaimed in glee, "this is it!"

Slade was mortified. He had been so excited and looking forward to his call with Michael! He'd been working on the big reveal in his Batman costume for months. Travis walking in during the call had been a nightmare. He kicked himself—he should've *known* his boyfriend would realize he was lying about being at the gym.

Then, something odd happened to his boyfriend as he video-bombed the call. He'd never seen Travis act so strangely and had barely taken it all in before the screen suddenly went dark as Michael abruptly ended the call.

Travis wasn't quite sure what had happened, either. He remembered walking in and starting to confront Slade about this … this … cosplay queen. But the next thing he knew the laptop's display was blank.

"I can't believe you stormed in here like that and embarrassed me!" Slade said, clearly upset.

But Travis had to admit that a furious Slade costumed as Batman was both unnerving and arousing at the same time. He shook his head. *No … no,* Travis thought, *I'm mad at him right now.* Travis glared at Slade, doing his best to look angry. "Look, I don't know what exactly is going on between you and that *guy,* but it ends now!"

Slade winced. "Babe …" he pleaded, "he's just an online crush, nothing more."

"My ass," Travis retorted, "I saw how you were mooning over him when I walked in! I know you too well, Mr. Bishop."

Uh-oh. Mr. Bishop—he was in deep shit. Slade contemplated how to claw his way out of this dilemma when his laptop dinged. He looked at the screen, where a message with a Batman symbol had popped up. Emblazoned across the screen was the message:

Congratulations Slade Bishop! You've been randomly selected for an all-expense paid trip for two to the San Diego Comic-Con! Pack your costumes and get ready for a stellar time! Check your email in the next few days for your travel itinerary.

"Hey! Wow! Look at this!" he turned the laptop so Travis could see the screen.

"OH LOVELY! And I bet that stinking Michael Hamm is going to be at that Con, isn't he?"

Slade said nothing.

"*Isn't he?*" Travis repeated. "Well, this is *perfect*. I'm going to go to that ridiculous Nerd-Con with you, Mr. Bishop. And I'm going to make it clear to this Michael Hamm that your little online romance is *over*."

Slade paled. "Travy, you can't be serious. I should probably just take one of my friends that are into cosplay, like Jake or ..."

"OH NO—and don't call me Travy! You're in the doghouse right now. We're going to San Diego together, and I'm going to make it a trip you and Mr. Hamm will *never* forget."

Slade gulped. He knew he was beat.

Travis triumphantly whirled around and marched out the door.

Slade walked into the bedroom, pulled off his cowl and looked in the mirror. "I bet Batman doesn't deal with this crap." Then he turned sideways and surveyed his reflection. "But damn! I do look good."

MINING
A HERO

"Damn it!" Michael tossed the small utility knife onto his worktable. He'd been working on the boots, archery bracer, and leg straps for his new Arsenal costume the past couple of days and wasn't making much progress. Over the past week, he'd had a rough time sleeping. The info Melodie shared had been both enlightening and maddening. He found himself dreaming over and over about Myriad, Melodie, Silas, the Inn, Beatriz, Travis, the pendant—it was all he practically thought about night and day. And, it was made worse by the fact he didn't have anyone to talk to about any of this.

He had to fly to San Diego in four days, and he had shit to get done if he was going to show up and make appearances that lived up to his picky standards.

He was tempted to contact the San Diego Comic-Con and cancel his trip and appearances altogether but fought the urge. If Myriad was going to be part of his life now, he needed to figure out how to balance this new secret hero identity with his public life as Michael Hamm, pro-cosplayer.

After a few more minutes of fiddling with his boots, he gave up. *I need to handle some of this built-up tension,* he decided. He left his workspace, went to his bedroom, threw his gym bag together, and headed out the door. Hopefully a good workout would help.

A half-hour later he was at the gym, and already felt better. Arsenal—and Tempest—both needed impressive guns, and he meant to deliver. Every chance to work out would help.

That reminded him—he needed to see if the Comic-Con folks had a makeup artist that could help him with Tempest's tribal-themed tattoos. This was good. He was focused on costumes, getting ready for the Con … this was a much better headspace. He smiled to himself in satisfaction.

He moved over to the rowing machines. *This will help beef up these shoulders,* he mused as he grabbed the oars. As he began working up a sweat, he made a mental list of the things he had to pack. He also had to ask his roomie about feeding Grayson and call his mom before he left.

While going through this mental and physical exercise, he glanced up at one of the TV screens. There was a breaking news story about a collapse at Kidd Mine—a copper mine located outside of Timmins, a small town in Ontario. The banner feed at the bottom of the screen read:

It is believed that eighteen mine workers are trapped inside the collapsed mineshaft.

Michael stopped rowing and grabbed his phone. He pulled up the report and turned the sound up on his earbuds. The reporter was saying:

"Experts are afraid to do any digging in the area until they have a chance to fully assess the mine and figure out the best way to reach the trapped workers. They could be stuck in there for days

before a rescue plan is fully developed, and there is great concern there isn't adequate oxygen in the shaft. Timmins is a small town with a tight-knit mining community. The families of the trapped are gathering now at the mine and, as you can imagine, are incredibly worried for their loved ones. We'll bring updates to you as soon as we get any new information."

Michael shuddered. He was claustrophobic and would be going out of his mind if he was stuck down in that shaft! He felt sorry for those miners and their families.

He put his phone down and started rowing again. Then, almost as soon as he had started, he stopped. *Wait a minute,* he realized, *this is the chance I've been waiting for. The chance to see if I can bring Myriad forth again!*

He hopped off the rowing machine, grabbed his stuff, and left the gym. *Well, this is tricky,* he thought. *I need to find a place to test this out and see if it works.* He walked around the outside of the gym but didn't really see an ideal hidden spot where he could secretly attempt an undetected transformation into Myriad.

He walked two blocks over where he knew there was a parking garage. He entered the first floor and looked around, then glanced up in the corner. Cameras ... ugh. Best not to have this on film in case it worked—or in case someone saw him and thought he was a nutcase.

He turned around to leave and saw a door that led to a stairwell. Ah-ha! Maybe...? He went through the door and up one flight of stairs. "Eeew ..." There was a stench in the stairway, and he'd rather not figure out its origin. But the light on the next landing was out; it was dim and isolated.

"Okay," he decided, "let's give this a try." He removed the pendant from his backpack and sat it on the first concrete step of the next flight.

Then, on a whim, he pulled out his phone and found a spot where he could record his transformation. *If this works, I wanna see what it looks like,* he thought. He hit record and positioned the phone. Then, he gave his best determined heroic pose and exclaimed, *"Myriad!"*

The tingling sensation he'd felt at the Inn began, and before he knew it, he was enveloped in that bright light. A few moments later, the light dissipated, and he was decked out in the blue, silver, and black costume, complete with mask and cape. *Wow. Just wow.* He wondered if he would get used to this feeling. He looked down at his chest to see the ruby red part of the "M" slightly glowing. It was then he realized that the garnet of the pendant must actually be embedded in the emblem, positioned to not only empower but protect him. That must also mean that Melodie was tucked away in the gem along for the ride to witness what transpired! He felt an increased sense of confidence knowing that she was accompanying him as his guardian angel.

Okay! He had successfully morphed into Myriad. But now he had to get to the mine, and time was of the essence. Timmins wasn't far outside of Toronto, which was about a forty-five-minute flight from Halifax. So, first order of business—he needed to fly to Timmins.

Fly… holy crap. "Okay … who do I draw from?" he said out loud. Then, as he grabbed his phone and put it away, he began listing heroes he'd cosplayed that possessed the power of flight: Shazam, Superboy of course, Hawkman, Green Lantern. *Well, Superboy is a fave, so let's go for it.* He headed up the stairs and exited at the top floor of the parking garage. He did his best launch pose and prepared for liftoff. This would be the first time he'd flown, and he didn't know exactly what to expect.

But … nothing happened! "What the hell?" he moaned. "Okay … don't panic. Think. We'll move on and give someone else a try. Hmm … Hawkman required Nth Metal—not sure if that can be conjured easily—or, for that matter, Green Lantern's ring. But I've got willpower to spare, so let's try a little Hal Jordan on for size."

He closed his eyes and imagined Green Lantern in his mind. When he opened them, he looked down and the red of his Myriad emblem had changed to emerald green and was glowing brightly. "Hot damn!" he exclaimed. He knelt, made a fist with his left hand, raised it toward the sky, and then leapt.

And he was floating in the air! He looked down. "Whoa—this will take some getting used to, but it seems to be working. Okay … off to Timmins!" He willed the power in the emblem to take him to Timmins, and he was enroute. He was somewhat wobbly, but after about five minutes Michael determined how to use the cape to level out his flight. "This is so fucking unbelievable!" he yelled out to the sky. There was still a lot to learn with this newfound ability and the mysteries not yet shared by Melodie, but he was going to have to figure out some of it on his own.

And it was incredibly exciting.

When he arrived in Timmins, he quickly spotted the mass of people gathered at the mine. He neared the site and made an attempt to slowly lower to the ground. But he didn't quite fully manage the landing before he made contact, which caused him to skip a couple of times and then unexpectedly nosedive. He did a somersault and landed back up on his feet. "Uhh … embarrassing." Michael looked around to see if anyone saw him, but everyone was intent on the entrance to the mine-shaft and they hadn't noticed his arrival.

Michael had to determine how he could try to save the miners without drawing attention. He wasn't exactly sure how he would field questions from bystanders. He quickly ran toward the back of the mine and took cover behind a huge boulder.

First, he needed to discover the location of the trapped miners. He willed the emerald power to scan the mine to find them. Kidd Mine was deep, and shaft #4—where the collapse had occurred—was well over 9,000 feet below the surface. The miners were at about the 6,500-foot spot in the mineshaft. The power he wielded enabled Michael to see the trapped miners. Most appeared to be standing or sitting upright, so they must be fine, but a few were on the ground as a couple men tended to them. Several clearly must have suffered some injuries during the accident.

Michael's adrenaline soared. God, he hoped he wasn't an idiot and could really help those people! After some indecision, he recognized that, given his powers were born of magic he should be able to do something. He didn't receive this gift on a fluke, according to Melodie. It was time to put his abilities to the test.

The scan also enabled him to see the weak spots in the mineshaft, pointing out the best place to break through on the other side of the collapse and not cause further damage.

How the hell was he going to get through the rock and earth to the safe space in the shaft? He looked down at the emblem's emerald glow. Uh ... great. The green light in his costume's emblem was fading, and the ruby glow was returning. There must be a time limit on tapping into the powers of his heroes.

He started flipping through a mental list of other characters and heroes he'd cosplayed over the years—*Aquaman, Robin, Batman, Iceman, Cyclops ... yes!* TERRA! Tara Markov had geokinesis—she could control and manipulate all forms of rock and earthly materials. She also had the ability to fly.

He stood on a nearby patch of solid earth and using both fists drew a block of it up under him. The ground rumbled and the patch dislodged under his feet, and he rose into the air. He could hear cries from the crowd in the distance. *Shit. They probably think there's an earthquake or something's happening in the shaft. I better make quick work of this.*

With the scan in mind, he flew toward the quarry. Concentrating, he slowly started boring his way through the earth. He kept digging, farther and farther through the rock and dirt. After about two minutes, he'd managed to make it all the way down to shaft #4 and broke through on the other side of the collapse.

He heard the muffled conversation of the trapped miners through the heap of rock and earth separating them. He directed his power and carefully dug a hole about the size of a dinner plate through the barrier and broke through. "Hello! Can you hear me in there?"

A bright light from a miner's hat filled the small tunnel he'd created, temporarily blinding him. Somehow his powers compensated, and he could see the man who had approached the opening. "We're here," the miner called. "Everyone is accounted for, but a few are injured. Do you have a way to get us out of here?"

Then, seeing Michael's masked face in the glow of his headlamp, he said, "Uh … wait a minute. How on earth did you get down here? And what's with the mask? Who the hell are you?"

"There will be time for that later," Michael replied. "I know what I'm doing, but you'll have to step back." He fervently hoped he *really* did know what he was doing.

He moved away from the opening he'd created and straightened his left arm forward and slowly started rotating it. As he did, the small opening got bigger and bigger. The earth and rock liquefied under his power and created a smooth tunnel large enough for the miners to pass through.

"Come on over!" Michael called. One by one, each of the men emerged on the other side of the collapse. The first few helped the injured, holding them up so they could limp through, and one was being carried by two of the men. "This guy isn't doing too hot," one of the men said. "He broke his femur, and I think he's bleeding internally. We need to get him out of here."

"He goes first, then," Michael said.

The miner looked at him blankly, then asked, "Goes where?"

Michael didn't reply. Instead, he focused on producing a stretcher from the rubble. The workers were awestruck. "Put him on this," Michael said. Once the man had been hoisted onto the makeshift stretcher, Michael flew the injured worker through the air and up out of the mine to the other side of the quarry near the entrance where the rescue party was working.

When they neared the crowd, one of the mine supervisors gasped, "My God, it's Frank. How did you get him out—and exactly who are you supposed to be?"

Michael gritted his teeth—getting a glimpse into why he had to keep Myriad under wraps until he could better handle these types of circumstances. "No time for questions, sir. I'm going to work at getting the rest of the trapped out of there. Be back soon!"

And with that, over the next thirty minutes, Michael slowly rescued every one of the trapped miners, delivering them safely back outside onto solid ground.

Relieved, he realized he wasn't quite yet done in the mine. He flew back inside and surveyed the shaft. Using geokinesis, he cleared the collapse and opened the shaft back up while strengthening the walls to ensure it wouldn't cave again. When he was satisfied, he flew back out and returned to the rescue party at the mine's entrance.

He walked over to the supervisor and explained what he'd done in shaft #4. "Don't worry," he concluded, "according to my calculations, the tunnel should be plenty strong for any work you need to do now and for a good long time."

"This is astonishing," the mine supervisor said. "How were you able to do all of this? Are you from another planet—like Superman or something?"

Michael laughed. "I'm afraid it's nothing that exotic," he said. "I'm just a Canadian."

Shit! He shouldn't have said that. *Idiot! You're making trouble for yourself that you don't have any idea how to handle.*

He called forth the block of earth he'd used to travel down into the mineshaft and quickly jumped onto it. "I'm off!" he called.

"Wait! Who are you? We don't even know your name!"

Michael hesitated briefly. If things continued in the direction he'd started out today, they'd undoubtedly want to know his name. Heaven forbid they started calling him *Kid Canada* or *Maple Boy* or something. He looked down from above and said, "It's *Myriad*. Take care everyone!" And with that he waved at the wondering crowd below and flew back to Halifax.

When he arrived in his hometown, it was getting dark. *Perfect,* Michael thought, *it will be easier to return to myself under the cover of darkness.* He'd landed on the top floor of the deserted parking garage and returned to the stairwell, grimacing at the smell again.

"Okay ... *Myriad!*" The light enveloped him and within moments he was back in his gym clothes. His backpack was at his feet and the pendant was on the concrete beside it. He picked it up and looked into the garnet, straining to get a glimpse of a tiny Melodie inside—nothing.

He sighed. "Melodie," he said, "I wish I could talk to you right now. I'd love to hear what else you were going to tell me! I hope you saw what just happened—it was pretty mind-blowing. And now ... people know about me. So, like it or not, Myriad's on the map."

He stored the pendant in his backpack, walked down the stairs, and headed home.

TWENTY-ONE

WESTWARD
BOUND

 Travis and Slade emerged from the jetway after deplaning at San Diego International and headed down to baggage claim. Once they retrieved their bags they'd head to the hotel where they would be staying while at San Diego Comic-Con.

Slade was both excited and terrified to be there. This was his first opportunity to be at the biggest Comic-Con out there for geeks like him. He never imagined that, not only would he be here, but with a Batman costume to show off AND a chance to meet Michael Hamm in person.

He was also nervous as hell after Travis's resolute determination to attend the Con with him and confront Michael. He had been wracking his brain to figure out how to convince Travis from challenging Michael and embarrassing him again. But nothing had come to mind.

He loved Travis but he didn't want to give up any opportunity to interact with the cosplayer. Travis had demanded that he end his Fandom support for Michael, but he'd persuaded his boyfriend to wait until Travis had some time to calm down. He'd tried to avoid any conversation that might lead to any mention of Michael. But now that they were here, that was going to be difficult.

Still, between trepidation and excitement, the latter was winning out. Here he was in San Diego! It was warm, they'd just enjoyed a flight in first class, a car was picking them up to take them to their free boutique hotel, which was blocks from the San Diego Convention Center, and they had tickets to the opening party! It all seemed like a dream. Slade just prayed it didn't turn into a nightmare.

Travis broke Slade's reverie by plopping his bags next to him. "Hey space cadet. I was talking to you! Here are your bags—you're welcome."

"Sorry babe," he replied and gave Travis a squeeze. "I'm just so excited to be here!"

His boyfriend shot him a warning look. "Just make sure your excitement is strictly about being at the convention, and not anything— or *anyone*—else."

Slade died a little inside. It was best not to reply to that statement. Travis would detect the lie.

"Hey look!" Slade pointed to a man holding a sign with the San Diego Comic-Con logo and his name in bold print below. "That must be the driver they sent to pick us up." He turned to Travis. "You *have* to confess this VIP treatment is just a little bit wonderful."

Travis sighed, "I admit it. And I know getting to the San Diego Comic-Con has been on your bucket list for years, so I'm happy you're getting such special treatment to boot. And," he said with satisfaction, "that of course you'll get to share it with me."

Ignoring any chance of going down the wrong path with Travis, he instead picked up his backpack and popped the handle on his bag. He beamed at his boyfriend and grabbed his hand. "Let's go!" No matter what lay ahead, Slade was convinced this was going to be a life-changing experience. He could feel it in his bones!

Michael emerged from the jetway after deplaning at San Diego International and headed to baggage claim.

He liked where he lived. He really did. But man! What he would give for Halifax to be closer to *anything* connected to the places he had to visit for his appearances. His travel had started at 7:00 a.m. that morning at Halifax International. The first flight had taken him to Toronto, then another flight to Atlanta, then finally to San Diego. It was now 10:20 p.m. and four time zones later. He still needed to get his bags and get to his hotel.

Fortunately, he had nothing to do tomorrow but adjust to the new time zone and explore the city before the convention started the following day. And his hotel was just a block and a half from the Comic-Con, which was terrific. And, because the city would be teeming with convention goers, his usual awkward feeling when walking down the street in costume would be at a bare minimum. He would still get plenty of looks, maybe a few catcalls or whistles, and fans that might stop him along the way for a photo op. But that was all part of a convention, and he was ready.

He had to admit, the events in Timmins had given him newfound confidence. He still had a lot to learn about Myriad, and he dearly hoped there would be another appearance from Marcel/Melodie soon. But he'd be arriving for the first time at a Con as not only a cosplay guest star but also as a new secret superhero! What a nerdy geek kid dream! That seven-year-old version of himself in Spider-Man jammies was bursting with excitement.

He was eager to debut a couple new looks for the convention. He'd finally managed to complete Arsenal and was happy with the result. He had Tempest to unveil as well. The convention team had connected him with a makeup artist to help with the tattoos to complete the look. He'd worked hard to get his body cosplay fit. He felt organized, ready, and set for what lay ahead.

He retrieved his bags and looked for the driver that should be there to meet him. After a few minutes, he saw the gentleman with the sign with his name displayed on it.

This was going to be a great Comic-Con. He could feel it in his bones!

Beatriz emerged from the jetway after deplaning at San Diego International and headed down to baggage claim. Matisse was resting comfortably in the cage he traveled in the few times Beatriz ventured away from New Orleans. "Don't fret, my little pet," she whispered, "we're almost to our destination." The African Gray shifted on the perch in his cage, signifying he'd heard his mistress's message.

After the dashed attempt to use Travis to siphon the garnet's power from such a great distance, the enchantress realized she'd need to be in closer proximity to succeed in recovering the mystic energy Michael now possessed. She despised the sun, and Californians—people in general were just too light and cheery for her. But the prize for her efforts far outweighed any discomfort from a trip like this.

She grabbed her bag and headed outside. She found the taxi stand to take a cab—she despised the ride app business. She gave the driver the address for the small apartment she'd rented from a local for the week. No hotel for her. Beatriz didn't need a bunch of people around or any interruptions—the fewer distractions, the better. She had to be on her toes, ready to sense when Travis was near Michael so she could again possess Eugenia's son and finally get back the power her ancestor had foolishly lost those many years ago.

She smiled to herself. The witch had to wait just a little longer. Success was hers. She could feel it in her bones!

TWENTY-TWO

REVELATION DAY ON THE BAY

Michael stepped onto the yacht in San Diego Bay. The first day of the Comic-Con had been fast-paced. He had been ferried by volunteers from one appearance to the next, to a photo session to an interview. Arsenal had been a hit, and he was feeling pretty good.

This whole opening party was a first. He figured that, since this was the return of the convention after the pandemic, they wanted to make a splash—literally. It was being held on a 140-foot superyacht! No doubt they had a few supporters with deep pockets willing to make the Con's return memorable. The yacht was stunning.

It was still about forty-five minutes before the party officially started. He had underdressed his new Tempest costume under his street clothes. He was scheduled to meet the makeup artist in one of the suites to get the tattoos done to complete the look and would then grab a bite to eat. Since he was going to be costumed as an aqua-themed hero for the event, one of the local TV stations reporting on the convention requested a quick interview with him as Tempest. They agreed to mention his Fandom page on the news and share the link. Great chance to increase his fan base!

"Michael! Over here!" He saw Steph, the liaison he was meeting. She would be escorting him to the suite. He waved and walked over to greet her.

She led him down into the superyacht's interior and delivered him to a richly appointed suite with a lovely seating area and a spacious bedroom where the makeup artist was waiting. "This is Lia. She's fab. She'll make you look great. Well, you already look great." Steph grinned and turned to Lia. "He's all yours."

Lia shook Michael's hand and showed him where to ditch his street clothes and store his backpack. Then he took a seat, and the makeup artist went to work. Fifteen minutes in, she let him go to the bathroom to view his full image. He looked in the mirror—it was awesome. As he checked out his reflection, he thought he heard his name. He looked around, thinking someone must have entered the suite's bedroom space outside the bathroom. But there was no one there.

He turned to head back to Lia's workspace. Then he heard his name again, this time more urgently. "Michael!" It was then he realized it was Marcel calling him.

"Marcel? Where are you? How can I hear you?"

"Somehow, I can reach you, which means there must be danger. Be careful!"

Michael turned back around and stared into the mirror. Danger, great, but what? And what kind of peril was brewing that was urgent enough for Marcel to break through from his isolation to warn him?

Lia's voice then called to him, "Michael, is everything okay? If it's not right, I can clean it off and start over."

"No, no—everything looks great. I'll be right there."

He returned to his seat and as he sat down, his head started to hurt a bit. *This can't be good,* he thought. "Hey Lia, do you know if there's any ibuprofen around? I seem to be developing a headache."

"I have some in my purse. I'll grab it."

She returned a few moments later with pills in hand and a glass of water.

"Thanks a lot, I really appreciate it." He downed the ibuprofen, hoping it was just a headache, nothing more. He grinned at Lia. "I'm all yours!"

After another twenty-five minutes, she had finished. He returned to the bathroom to take another look. It was fantastic. *I wish I could have a professional makeup artist on call all the time. Damn, that would be so cool.*

He thanked Lia for her help, and they took a selfie together, which she texted to him. "I have a few friends that will be sooo jelly," she smiled.

"Aw … that's nice to hear." Just then Steph reentered the suite and told Michael things were getting underway up top. He dutifully followed her to his designated spot to sign autographs and for photo-ops. The area was set up on the aft. A bar had been placed at the center, with tables lining each side near the yacht's rail for the onboard cosplay guests. Small lines were already queuing up with anxious fans.

Soon the entire yacht was humming. A DJ was spinning music and twilight descended. After about forty-five minutes of fan interaction, he spotted Steph approaching his spot.

"How's it going?" she asked.

"Things have been great!" And they really had been. Short of the still nagging headache, everything was going really well. It was turning out to be a great night.

"Awesome!" Steph turned to the folks still waiting. "Hey everyone—unfortunately, I have to steal Michael for about a half-hour for a TV interview. But he'll be back at 8:30 after a short break. We'll mark your places in line so when he returns you'll start right where you left off, cool?" The crowd moaned slightly, and then spoke with the other volunteer recording their spots in line before they peeled off to take in the rest of the festivities.

She turned to Michael. "The reporter wants to interview you in front of the hot tub, since you're costumed as Tempest. I'll take you over, then after you wrap, you can retreat to the suite for some food and a break."

"Sounds good," Michael said as he followed Steph, winding their way through the crowd. Everyone was in such a good mood, being courteous, saying hello, and complimenting him on his costume and makeup. They arrived near the hot tub and Steph introduced Michael to the reporter, Jamison French. *That's got to be made up,* Michael thought. He nevertheless smiled, shook his hand, and let Jamison explain what he hoped to cover during the segment.

A few minutes into the interview he'd started to answer a question about if he normally crafted versus purchased his costumes. But before he had a chance to finish, his headache suddenly became worse, and he flinched at the pain.

Jamison said, "Are you doing okay there, pal?"

Realizing they were still on camera, Michael put on a brave face and said, "I'm great—just a little headache."

He returned his focus to the reporter. His head was getting worse. *Something's wrong.* Just then, behind Jamison, he saw Slade walking toward them. *Oh my God—what is he doing here?* Then, he saw Travis was accompanying him.

Travis. Shit—that's the cause of the pain. I need to get out of here. Michael interrupted Jamison and said, "Gosh, I hate to do this, but I've got to get something for this headache. I have a really long night ahead! Thanks so much for wanting to talk with me." He looked at the camera and smiled, then waved, and turned around.

"Hey! Michael … it's me, Slade! Surprise!"

Michael didn't turn but instead searched for a way to escape Slade and his boyfriend. He darted in and out of the crowd until he found the stairway to the interior suite where he'd been stationed earlier. A staff member from the yacht was just finishing up a delivery of fruit and other munchies. "Thanks for this, it's great." Michael smiled and ushered him out of the suite and shut and locked the door. He grabbed his backpack from where he'd stored it and felt for the pendant. Retrieving it, he ran into the bathroom.

The minute he did so, the pendant glowed, and the ruby flash shot to the mirror. Melodie was in plain view.

"They're here," Michael said breathlessly. "This is a nightmare. How am I going to deal with them on a crowded yacht?"

"Don't panic, honey," Melodie said soothingly, "you got this. We'll figure it out together. I'm here to help you as best I can."

Just then there was a knock at the door. "Michael, are you in there? It's me, Slade."

"And his boyfriend Travis—I'm *dying* to meet you. Come on out."

Michael looked at Melodie alarmingly. "Holy shit—this is not good. I'm trapped in here!"

"No, you're not. Think for a minute," Melodie said. "They're clearly here for another round of 'get the garnet'. That's not going to happen if I have anything to say about it. Now, the first order of business—we need Myriad."

"Myriad … of course! I'm so stupid!" He uttered the name of his hero identity and suddenly was staring at his reflection in the mirror in real superhero mode.

"Hey, you two can't be down here," a voice boomed, speaking to Slade and Travis outside the door. "If you want to see Michael, he'll be back topside in about twenty minutes."

Travis started objecting, but Slade managed to convince him to head back upstairs.

"Thank God!" Michael turned back to the mirror. "Now what?"

Melodie cleared her throat. "Michael, with all due respect sweetie, you need to get a grip. You've handled this superhero thing well so far, and this will be no different."

"That's easy for you to say! Up till now the only time Myriad's been in action was to save people. This time is different. I feel like this is the showdown."

Melodie didn't mince words. "It is; I'm not going to lie. But you need to listen very carefully. You have the power and the self-confidence to do this, as well as the smarts to outwit them. And you also have our bloodline, which is something that witch Beatriz doesn't realize. It's our ace in the hand, if you will."

"*Our bloodline*—what exactly does that mean?"

"It's what I meant to tell you before our last encounter ended so quickly. When my ancestors arrived in America, my Grandmama Marie headed to New Orleans. But her husband, Benjamin, had business to attend to in Canada. So, he arrived in Boston and traveled up to Halifax."

Michael eyes widened, then stammered, "Uh ... he went to Halifax?"

Melodie pulled out a nail kit and began filing and polishing her nails. "Yes, he had interests in textiles, and when they left Europe textile factories were springing up like mad in your hometown. He intended to take make investments in two of the factories under construction. And while he was there ... well ... he partook in a dalliance with one of the locals. More specifically, he had sex with someone in your family tree. So ..." Melodie blew on her nails observing her handiwork, then looked pointedly at Michael, "we are all related—you, me, and Travis."

I'm ...I ..." Michael stuttered. "Well, this seems absolutely insane!" He looked at the emblem glowing on his chest. "So—this garnet ..."

"... is as much yours as it is mine," Melodie finished. "And that's why you were able to reactivate the spell and tap into the power. Now we need to beat that miserable witch and destroy her hold over Travis so you're free to fully possess the complete power of the garnet—and the power of Myriad."

TWENTY-THREE

THE SHOWDOWN
MUST GO ON

 Beatriz found a bench with generous shade under a carrotwood tree in Bayside Park and settled in for the wait.

She despised water. But with the Comic-Con opening party on the superyacht in the distance, she might need to brave heading out onto the bay if she couldn't gain enough control over Travis when it was time to perform her siphoning spell. She'd identified a man with a small motorboat close by and paid him a tidy sum in case that was necessary.

"Time to collect! Time to collect!" Matisse squawked next to Beatriz on the bench, pecking away at a handful of cashews and sunflower seeds she'd scattered beside her.

"Very true, my pet—our prize is almost in hand." The witch reached into her oversized satchel and retrieved her crystal ball. She rubbed it and whispered a few magical words. Soon the reflection in the orb revealed Travis and Slade on the yacht. She watched them intently until Slade called out Michael's name.

"Excellent!" she cackled. "They've found that miserable Canuck." She had to resist the urge to try and fully possess Travis too early. She didn't want to give away that she was nearby ready to mount an attack and seize the garnet's magic. But the enchantress decided to attempt a quick test possession to determine if she was still too far away to accomplish what lay ahead. She whispered the word to activate the siphoning spell—"*Dairym.*"

In a split second she realized that she'd been unsuccessful. "Damn it!" Beatriz returned the crystal ball safely inside her satchel and gathered up Matisse, placing him back in his cage. "Sorry pet, much as I hate to do so, it appears we're going to have to take a little trip on the water after all."

She walked over to the spot where Mr. Castonetti's boat was moored. The Italian was sitting on the dock, legs dangling, smoking a cigar, and taking in the view.

He greeted Beatriz as she approached. "Ah ... the lady needs a ride I take it?"

"Yes, the lady does, Mr. Castonetti."

He hopped into the boat and reached out his hand. "Allow me—and please, call me Antony."

Beatriz mumbled, "Very well," and handed him Matisse's cage, then allowed him to assist her onboard. Just the gentle rocking made her feel squeamish. But she had to forge ahead; she was too close to let anything get in her way now.

Beatriz pointed out into the bay. "I need to get closer to that yacht. Can you manage that?"

Antony grinned broadly. "Why of course, *signorina.*" He started the engine, the motor roared, and he pointed the boat in the direction of the superyacht.

Slade was grazing near one of the tables covered with finger foods for the party guests. Travis was idly sipping his drink. Occasionally he'd glance at the stairs to the interior, hoping to see Michael emerge. He was intent on meeting and confronting Michael. Oddly enough, he couldn't quite put his finger on *why* exactly this was so important. Yes, he did want to meet the cosplayer and make it clear that Slade was taken. And yes, he was well aware he was thinking illogically about Slade being overly obsessed with the Canadian. Still, he needed to get this out of his system.

Slade was obliviously enjoying himself. He was surveying the other guests, appreciating the many that were in costume for the party. He had wanted to show up in one of his costumes (not Batman—that was for the convention floor). But there was no way he'd give his boyfriend the chance to tease him in front of the other attendees. It would be innocent fun to Travis, but it would be uncomfortable and embarrassing for Slade if any of the passersby overheard. He'd resorted to just wearing a Batman T-shirt that impressively hugged his torso and biceps.

He was really hoping to talk to Michael tonight. He wanted to know if the cosplayer was planning to wear Nightwing or Robin this week. If yes, he wanted to find out what day so he could get some photos of him decked out as the Dark Knight with Michael as one of his sidekicks. *That* would be icing on the cake for him on this trip. But he needed to keep that under wraps, so Travis didn't have a meltdown.

He was still lost in thought when Travis grabbed his arm. "Look!" he whispered, "there's Michael! He just came up and he's trying to slip around to the other side of the boat, no doubt to avoid us."

Slade looked at him. "Uh, first, why are you so intent on seeing Michael tonight? He'll be here all week. And second ..." he looked in the direction Travis had pointed, "I don't see Michael anywhere."

"Ugh," Travis started pulling his boyfriend by the hand through the crowd, "sometimes you can be so dense! Come on—I don't want to lose him."

"Hey!" Slade protested as his boyfriend dragged him from behind. "What is going on with you?"

Travis didn't reply. He was going to find that Canadian. He wouldn't be able to get rid of this mysterious nagging feeling until he did. Just then, the crowd parted, and Travis saw Michael, his back turned to them. He no longer wore that Tempest costume, but Travis knew without a doubt the cosplayer was in his sights. And this time he wasn't going to lose him. At that moment, Travis's body stiffened, and his eyes took on a sinister gaze. "You!" he cried out. But it wasn't his voice that called to Michael, it was Madam Beatriz's.

TWENTY-FOUR

Siphon Makes a Splash

The minute he heard the witch's voice, Michael felt an explosion of pain. Cradling his head between his hands, he slowly turned. Struggling to stay on his feet, he nevertheless willed himself to do so and managed to say, "Game's up, Beatriz. I know it's you."

For a moment, Travis looked shocked, but then quickly recovered. "Oh—you think you're so smart, and that's all very well. But I promise you that before the night's over I'll have what I'm after and you may—or may not—be alive to see it."

Slade was watching just a few feet away. He didn't understand why Travis was behaving so erratically or why his voice had taken on this odd quality. He also didn't know who this guy was he was talking to, and the costume was entirely unfamiliar. He stepped forward and started, "Travy, maybe you've had more to drink than I thought. Perhaps we should call it a night."

Travis whirled around and Beatriz spat, "Get away from me you idiot. I'm not going anywhere until I succeed in my quest." Suddenly, the onyx in the ring that Beatriz had placed on Travis's finger and cast a spell on weeks ago became animated. The onyx began rising off the ring like a thin wispy rope. Then, the witch directed Travis's hand back and flung it forward. The black tendril slithered through the air and struck Slade in the chest. His eyes opened wide, and he collapsed, unconscious.

By now, the crowd realized something was going on and several had witnessed the attack. Many screamed and started running. But, of course, in the day of cell phones and social media, others pulled out their devices and started recording.

Michael watched as these events unfolded in front of him and reeled from the pain in his head. *I've got to get it together,* he thought. *We've got to get away from this crowd.* Before he could think any further, the black tendril from the ring began to wrap itself around Travis, fully enveloping him. Once he was completely covered in onyx, the black that had cocooned him shattered and fell to pieces to the deck.

Michael watched transfixed—Travis was now decked out in a costume of Beatriz's making. A dark green spandex suit covered his body from the neck down. Black boots, a black Moto-style leather jacket, and tight short black leather gloves finished the outfit.

Oh man, this can't be good. Michael wracked his brain about what to do next, and how to get Travis away from these party guests. Hopefully Slade was okay. He needed to make sure no one else got hurt.

Beatriz's voice spoke again, "My little pawn Siphon is ready to do his job and get me what I'm after."

Now a few emboldened partygoers moved closer. *Shit,* Michael thought, *some of these ding dongs must think this is some kind of entertainment. What the hell am I supposed to do?*

"Jump." Michael recognized the voice—it was Marcel's, inside his head.

"Jump—what are you talking about?"

"Michael, you have to get him somewhere isolated where we can figure out how to defeat Beatriz and make sure no one gets hurt. We need to get off this boat. JUMP."

"Dammit! Okay—I guess we're going to put Tempest to use in more ways than one tonight." With that Michael leapt into the air and dove over the side of the boat. As he did, his cape vanished and he pierced the water, disappearing into the bay.

Siphon cried out, "No!" and ran to the rail. Beatriz possessed Travis but didn't know everything about him. Especially that he wasn't a very good swimmer and had a fear of drowning.

Michael resurfaced from his dive. "Okay, Siphon, if you want me, you're going to have to come get me." He could see his new nemesis hesitating.

"You've got to get him off that boat before he does anything stupid and decides to hurt someone or takes a hostage," Marcel ordered.

"Great, how exactly am I going to do that?"

Marcel coached him, "You can do it honey. Just think of whose powers you can draw from and get him off that boat—*now*."

"God, I wish my head would stop hurting. Okay … think …" Michael started ticking off heroes he'd cosplayed. Then it struck him—he thought of Reed Richards, and then reached his left hand in Siphon's direction. His powers cooperated, and his arm stretched the unbelievable distance from where Michael floated in the water to where Siphon still stood on deck. Michael wrapped his arm around Siphon, lifted him up, and pulled him back toward him. The villain screamed (definitely the witch's scream) and hit the water.

After a few seconds, Siphon's head emerged, sputtering and flailing his arms. "Somebody help me!"

"Not gonna happen," Michael said. He quickly thought of his cape, and it reappeared. Before Siphon could say another word, Michael had wrapped the cape entirely around him so he couldn't struggle. Then, he used Tempest's aquatic powers and swam away from the yacht with Siphon in tow.

Once he'd tapped into Tempest, he was able to divine every sea creature, as well as the location of any surrounding islands. Michael sped toward the Channel Islands. He found San Miguel, one of the small isles with no population. They reached the shore and he flung Siphon still in the cape onto the sand, and then slowly pulled himself out of the water. Michael willed his cape to return to him, spinning Siphon out of it.

When Travis was pulled overboard, Beatriz had to take matters into her own hands. Mr. Castonetti was contentedly circling the yacht. She was likely going to get seasick at some point, but she had no choice. Without a word she pushed Antony overboard, who cried out in surprise just before he hit the water. He surfaced spitting and spewing a litany of Italian the witch couldn't understand.

Ignoring his protests, she grabbed hold of the wheel and set off in the direction Myriad had sped off with Siphon. She had no idea how long it would take to get wherever the Canadian had taken him, but she had to get close enough to regain control and seize the garnet's magic. And once she did, she was going to take out all her built-up anger on Myriad.

Travis sat up, stunned. He looked at his legs splayed in front of him, and then looked at his arms. "What the hell am I wearing?" he said aloud. Then he saw Michael. "Who are you? Where are we—what's happening?"

From inside Michael's head, Marcel said, "The witch has lost control over him. This is your chance. You must tell him what Beatriz is trying to do before she takes possession of him again—if she even can. The more we can impart, the greater your chances are at defeating her."

With the enchantress no longer controlling Travis, Michael's head had stopped throbbing. He heard Marcel loud and clear. With renewed energy and focus, he turned to Travis and recapped the story of the garnet, what had happened to Travis, and what Madam Beatriz intended to do.

Travis got up and brushed off his costume. He looked down at the silver and onyx ring on his gloved hand, then looked at Myriad. "This sounds too preposterous to be true."

Michael returned, "It is true. I wish it wasn't, and I have no desire to fight you. But if that witch has a chance to possess you again, I won't have a choice. You must do your best to remember everything I've told you and fight her yourself. It's the only way I think we can stop her—and keep us both alive."

Travis gulped; this explained why he'd been having memory lapses. A thought suddenly struck him. He vaguely remembered some of what he'd been forced to do on the yacht. "Oh God—did I do something to Slade? Is he okay??"

"Well, you didn't, Beatriz did, although she did it using you. I know you wouldn't do anything to hurt Slade, but you really had no way to resist. I'm sure he's alright. Even possessed, I don't think you could really hurt someone that you know and love."

Travis looked out over the water. "We have to get out of here. You need to take me back to that boat right now!"

Michael walked over to him and said gently, "Look, I know you're worried. But I can't really do that unless we figure out how to permanently break that witch's spell. Until then, the danger is too great."

Travis's eyes teared up. Then he looked down at the ring on his finger. "If this is gone, maybe her hold over me will be too." He attempted to pull it off his finger, but it wouldn't budge. He tugged and tugged, but it didn't move. "Damn it!" he cried.

Michael put his arm around him, then said softly, "We're going to figure this out, I promise. It's going to … *aaahhh!*"

Michael felt Travis's body go rigid as the pain in his head returned. He pushed Slade's boyfriend away and staggered back a few steps and looked into Travis's eyes.

Siphon had returned.

TWENTY-FIVE

FAMILY FEUD

Beatriz was frustrated. She had a very basic understanding of how to navigate a boat. Her father used to own one for his fishing business in the bayou. She had never been interested in going out with him—especially after, at a young age, she'd discovered she did not do well on the water. After driving for about fifteen minutes, the enchantress was doing fairly well steering the boat and making gradual progress reaching her destination.

But her body was not cooperating. She had to stop twice to throw up, which was affecting her ability to focus. Now idling, the boat drifted in the bay. Beatriz realized there was no way to bridge the gap between her and Travis. She looked in despair at Matisse in his cage. Having her victory slip through her grasp after all her planning was a hard pill to swallow.

Then, like a lightning bolt, the solution struck. She chastised herself aloud, "Seriously witch—what is *wrong* with you? All this time on this wretched boat was totally unnecessary. Matisse can be my conduit and fly close enough to Travis to reactivate the possession spell."

She pulled a small book from her satchel and located the conduit spell. It only took a few minutes to enchant Matisse. She released the bird, giving him instructions to get close enough to Travis so she could regain control of him. He squawked in reply and headed off in the direction of San Miguel.

When Matisse arrived on the island, he found a perch in a nearby tree where he was close enough to help his mistress. He watched the Canadian writhe in agony as the spell he carried for his mistress allowed her to overtake Travis, possessing him once more.

Siphon watched Michael with an amused look as the hero continued to back away holding his head in pain.

"Well, you thought you had escaped me, didn't you?" Again Beatriz's voice had replaced Travis's. "You're not going to get off that easily, you slippery snake. You have something I want, and I aim to finally get it."

As Michael watched Siphon, trying to figure out his next move to defeat the villain, the black tendril that had assaulted Slade on the yacht began flowing out of the onyx ring on Siphon's finger. He extended his arm toward Michael, willing the slithering ribbon of ebony in his direction. Before Michael could do anything, the villain drew his arm back and snapped it forward. The floating onyx reacted and attacked Myriad, hitting the space where the garnet was invisibly embedded in the emblem on his chest.

Michael fell backward, clenched his eyes shut and let out a piercing scream. The pain was nothing like he'd ever experienced in his life. He felt as if his life force was being drawn out of his body and transferred to Siphon. He pushed his eyes open a slit. He could see the garnet's magic was being leeched from the gem, traveling over the onyx ribbon and absorbed by Travis.

The witch laughed a villainous laugh. "Finally!" she said. "Finally, I will have the power and wealth that I should have had ages ago."

Another wave of unbelievable pain ravaged Michael's body as he cried out in agony again. He gritted his teeth and tried to rip the onyx connecting him to Siphon from his chest to no avail. *My God ... the pain ... Marcel ... help me ... what can I do?*

A bright flash of light answered Michael's urgent plea. Despite the pain, he heard Marcel's voice, "I'm here! We'll stop him together."

Somehow, in that instant, Melodie had broken free of the garnet and leapt from the ruby glow emanating from the emblem on Myriad's costume. She was standing beside Michael in her blue sequined glory.

"Holy shit!" Michael cried out. "How did you get here?"

Melodie didn't answer his question. Instead she said, "Grab my hand!"

Beatriz studied her crystal ball, watching in shock from the boat miles away on the bay. "What is this?" She jumped to her feet, forgetting she was on the boat, and nearly toppled overboard. She quickly sat down and grabbed the orb. It was *true*. Somehow that drag queen had materialized from the past and was standing united with the Canadian to battle Siphon.

She shook her head angrily. "No, no, no, I'm too close. I've got to find a spell to stop this." She picked up her satchel and frantically flipped through the pages of her spell book.

Back on San Miguel, Michael tried to comprehend what was happening. He fought through the pain and reached out to grab Melodie's extended hand.

Melodie looked at him and said, "You can do this. *We* can do this. We can stop him, together. Gather up all your willpower and deflect his attack!"

"I'll … try …" Michael stared straight at the villain and mustered his best aggressive stance through the searing pain. He looked at Melodie, and said, "Attack!"

They both ran toward Siphon, still doing his best to maintain the power drain from the garnet. Siphon faltered at the sudden appearance of the drag queen and the realization it was now two against one just as Melodie and Myriad tackled him. The villain fell to the ground and the ebony ribbon shattered and disappeared.

The pain Michael had been suffering ceased. His head was still throbbing, but it was a marked improvement over how he'd felt moments ago, and he felt his strength returning. The drag queen helped him up and they both stood facing Travis, still on the ground.

Melodie looked at Eugenia's son and said softly, "Travis, I know you're in there. You must break free from that witch's curse. Deep down, you've always wanted a chance to help your mother find me, and here I am. We need to end this and get you back to Slade and New Orleans."

For a brief moment, Siphon's eyes fluttered. Michael could see that Travis was managing to break through somehow. "Travis, are you there? We want to help you, but you've got to help us too. Stop her! End this!"

Then Melodie said, "We're all family here, all three of us. If we want to survive, we must end this family feud forced upon us."

Travis looked up at them and slowly got to his feet. "Marcel … how can you be here? I can't believe any of this … I don't know how to fight her … I'm not that strong …"

Michael and Melodie both gasped and retreated a few steps.

An apparition of Beatriz rose up behind Travis. In a split second, Marcel's great-nephew's eyes glazed over, and the witch was again in control of Siphon. This time, it was Beatriz's floating image that spoke. "This has gone on long enough! I'm not only going to finish what I started, but I'm going to finish both of you off while I'm at it." She glared at Melodie. Then, the ring on Siphon's finger glowed white hot and a black beam shot from it in Michael's direction.

"Nooo!" Melodie's cry started somewhere from deep inside and reached a fever pitch as she threw herself in front of Michael into the path of the ebony blast. It struck the drag queen in the chest and then there was another white flash of light, similar to the one that very first night when the magic had protected Melodie. The bright light ricocheted, sending the black beam back at Siphon smacking him squarely in the chest. The ring on Siphon's finger exploded into tiny pieces. Travis fell to the ground unconscious, and the witch's apparition screamed, and then she and her bird disappeared.

TWENTY-SIX

TRANSITIONS

The series of events happened so quickly Michael barely had a chance to take it all in. When Melodie had jumped in front of him intercepting Siphon's blast, the throbbing in his head finally dissipated. And Michael felt a new surge of power coursing through him. He looked down at the emblem on his chest. The ruby glow was brighter than it had ever been. He felt stronger and more powerful than when he'd first discovered the pendant at the Stonewall Inn.

Then, out of the corner of his eye, he saw Melodie lying prone on the ground. "Oh my God—Melodie!" He pulled off his cape and ran over to her. He rolled it up into a makeshift pillow, and then gently placed it under the drag queen's head. "How can I help? Tell me what you need."

Melodie opened her eyes and said weakly, "Dear sweet boy. I need nothing. I've done what I needed to do, and it's time for me to go."

"No!" Michael felt tears stinging his eyes. "We just made it to the other side of this. You can't leave now!"

Melodie turned toward Travis, who was starting to stir. She noted that Siphon's costume had disappeared with the witch, and his great-nephew was again in his normal clothes. She reached her hand out toward Travis, beckoning him to her. "Travy ... please come here."

Travis was still shaky. Now that Beatriz's curse was broken, he realized what her plan was and how she had used him as her unwitting pawn. He managed to crawl over to his great uncle. It was gut wrenching hearing Marcel call him by his mother's pet name, knowing what had just happened.

"I'm here," Travis said. "I'm so, so sorry."

Melodie shook her head briefly. She reached up and removed her wig, then nestled back into Myriad's cape. "Ah, that's better. I want you to tell your mother how grateful I am that she never gave up looking for me. Tell her that it's okay, and I'm now in a better place."

"Why are you talking like this? Myriad will get us out of here. We'll get you to a hospital."

Melodie shook her head again and smiled. "The two of you ... so sweet but so oblivious. I don't belong here. I don't belong in this time. Now that the garnet's power has been made whole, my job here is through. My responsibility was to get the small bit of magic that Beatriz's ancestors had held onto all this time that should have ended up with our family. That and the small bit that remained with me are now with Myriad, where it belongs."

He turned to Michael, then shared, "Now that you have full control of the garnet's mystic gift, the few glitches you experienced tapping into a hero or having the power fade after a time is through. You need to carry on and do something amazing with our family's magical heritage. You have the power, the strength and—most importantly—the self-confidence and pride to create your own legacy."

Michael brushed away tears and said, "This is too much all at once. You just got here." He looked at Travis, then back at Marcel. "I didn't know it till now, but I need you. We *both* need you."

Marcel winced and sighed weakly, then replied, "Soon enough you'll understand I've done all I can. You're both strong enough to carry on and live your lives as you were meant to. I know you'll both do great things and make me proud." He then turned to Michael one last time. "Please … tell Silas everything. My dear friend has a right to know. And both of you—be spectacular!"

Then, the life energy of Marcel DuPris and Melodie Monnaie floated away, and seconds later, his body disappeared.

Michael and Travis sat on the sand for quite some time.

It was now nearly dark. Instinctively Michael thought of Northstar and drew forth light to illuminate the area around them.

Travis looked at him. "Wow, that's really cool. Do you know everything you can do yet?"

Michael shook his head. "Not really. I've been figuring it out along the way, partially with your great uncle's help." He looked out at the bay. "Now I guess I'm on my own."

In a small voice, Travis said, "I'm sorry for what I did."

Michael looked at him and grabbed his hand, saying, "Don't be silly. You had no control over the part you played. We both need to move on and honor Marcel's wishes and be spectacular."

Travis got up and said, "I need to get back to Slade. God only knows what I'm going to tell him."

Michael stood, joining him. "You'll figure something out. Maybe …" he teased, "you can tell him you're getting him a lifetime membership to my Fandom page."

"Hilarious. Well, let's just say I'm going to be a lot more understanding about his fascination with you. Turns out you might be worthy of the attention."

Michael hugged Travis, then tapped into Northstar's ability to fly. He lifted them both off the ground and headed back to the yacht. When they reached the boat, the party was still going on as if nothing had happened.

Myriad flew them to the secluded cabintop to keep their arrival from attracting any unwanted attention. He looked at Travis and said, "We need to talk about …" Michael swept his hand up and down his costume, "… all this."

Travis held up his hand. "There's no need. I'll never reveal your secret, even to Slade. That's the least I can do in my great uncle's memory, and to show my gratitude."

Michael breathed a sigh of relief. "Thank you. I appreciate that."

Travis located Slade who seemed to be relatively unphased by what had happened earlier. He was dancing on deck near the DJ booth. He lit up when he saw Travis. "Hey hon! Where the hell have you been?"

"Are you okay? I saw you get hurt earlier."

Slade acted as if the prior events hadn't happened. Maybe the witch had erased the attack. "Huh? I'm fine. Now where did you disappear to? I looked and looked."

"I … found Michael and we hid ourselves away. We had a very long chat. Let's just say I was wrong about him."

Slade pulled him close and gave him a kiss. "I *knew* you'd come around! Let's dance."

After Travis had left, Michael whispered, "Myriad," and soon he was costumed as Tempest once again. While still emotionally shaken from what had happened and Marcel's passing, he knew he had to forge ahead. So, he made his way down to the suite. He located Steph and made apologies for his temporary disappearance, telling her he had to deal with his headache before he could continue with the night. Fortunately, the volunteer had been able to delay a couple of his final obligations. Grateful he didn't need to explain anything further, he let Steph take him to his next commitment for the evening.

FULL CIRCLE

Michael knocked on the door of Silas's brownstone in Brooklyn. It was a brilliant morning in early September. He'd wanted to get to New York sooner to share the events of his San Diego trip in July with Silas. Part of the reason it took until now was the cosplayer's busy schedule. But deep down the main reason was that Michael dreaded relaying what had happened to his dear friend from the Stonewall Inn.

Marcel had told him to tell Silas *everything*. Did that mean telling him about Myriad as well? That part hadn't been really clear. Michael had contemplated this non-stop the days leading up to his visit. But he still wasn't sure what he should reveal.

Silas opened the door, looking smart in khakis, sandals, and a crisply ironed flower print shirt. "Michael!" he opened his arms and Michael accepted his embrace. The moment he was in Silas's arms, he could feel tears on the way. He forced them back. *Don't get all weepy at the beginning, or you'll never make it through.*

Silas led him to the back patio where they had brunched several months ago. Fresh mimosas were waiting at the table. They each took their respective seats. Silas told Michael about a new musical he'd seen on Broadway two weeks ago, and updated him on the progress of rebuilding Stonewall. "It's been moving faster than they hoped," he concluded. "It's good to see that so many rallied around the landmark to make it whole again. They hope to be reopened in time for Halloween. You know, that gay holiday." Then he looked at Michael. "Although, I imagine for someone in your profession it is Halloween almost any day of the year."

The cosplayer smiled wanly, acknowledging the tease.

Silas noted his reaction and said, "Is something going on, dear?"

"I did want to come see you earlier, but I just couldn't manage it. I have some news to share—about Marcel."

"Oh, I see." Silas stared out into the backyard. Two of his neighbor's kids had just bounded outside and down the stairs with a soccer ball and began kicking it around. He looked back at Michael. "I had a feeling when you said you were coming to visit that it wasn't entirely social."

Michael shifted in his seat and took a sip of his mimosa. "I was sincere when I said I wanted to keep in touch. And it's really good to see you. But I do need to tell you about my trip to San Diego in July. You're going to think I've gone mad when I tell you everything, but now that I'm here, I know it's the right thing to do. Marcel told me as much before … well, I think you should get another drink. This is going to take a while."

"Told you …?" Silas questioned but then didn't say another word. He just rose from his chair and disappeared into the kitchen. He emerged a few minutes later with a huge glass filled to the brim with a Bloody Mary and freshly baked muffins. He downed a more than significant amount of his drink, then picked up his napkin, and dabbed his lips. "Okay … hit me."

When Silas said that, it was as if a floodgate had been released in Michael. He started with his visit to New York in June and filled in the parts he'd omitted previously about what happened to him when he found Melodie's pendant at the Inn. From there, he relayed everything that had transpired since. At one point, when Michael reached the part about Melodie appearing in Michael's bedroom mirror, Silas held up his hand. "One moment," he said, "I'm going to need another drink. Or two."

Silas again retreated into the kitchen. This time he DID return with two drinks in hand. He took a big swig of one of them, and then said, "Continue."

Forty-five minutes later, Michael finally explained how Melodie had leapt in front of him, breaking Beatriz's spell and rescuing Myriad. Once he finished, they both sat in silence for at least ten minutes. Then, they hugged each other fiercely and both took a moment to brush away the tears that had started flowing.

Michael reached down into his backpack and retrieved Melodie's purse. He placed it on the table and pushed it toward Silas. He said softly, "I had hoped to return this to your friend if I ever managed to break the curse and free him. Sadly that wasn't to be. But I believe in my heart this should be with you."

Silas placed his hand on the sequined bag, fingering the clasp absentmindedly, clicking the bag open, then shut, open, then shut again. Then he sighed. "Marcel was something. He was bold, proud, flamboy-ant ..." He looked at Michael and said wryly, "He thought he was a good singer, but we knew better."

They both laughed a little and took another sip of their drinks.

"But he regretted deeply that he had distanced himself from his family. I bet the discovery you two were related and his chance to see Travis meant a lot."

Michael nodded. His mind wandered back to his final moments with Melodie. "I could feel that from him when ... when he was in my arms."

Silas wiped a tear away and said, "So, all of this magical mystical Myriad stuff is real? You're secretly a superhero now?"

"Well, the jury's out on that one. I mean, yes, the Myriad stuff is true. But as for being a superhero—I've still got to figure all that out."

Silas tried to lighten the mood, musing, "You know, I've never seen Michael Hamm the professional cosplayer in costume in the flesh ... and I bet this old queen would be impressed—VERY impressed."

Michael laughed, "You are naughty. And you've had too much to drink."

"Can you blame me? You didn't exactly come to play a game of canasta. Tabloids would salivate over this story."

Canasta? Michael thought. *What the hell is that?*

Silas then grabbed his hand and pulled him up from his chair. "Come on."

Michael followed him into the brownstone. "Where are we going?"

Silas led him to the living room, positoned Michael in the center, and sat down on the sofa. "Oh! Wait a minute." He got up again, circled the room and closed the blinds, then turned on the overhead light.

"Uh ... what's going on?"

Silas crossed his legs and sat back. "Show me."

Michael realized what he was talking about. He sighed. "Okay, prepare yourself—and don't faint or anything."

Silas taunted, "Why, won't you rescue me?" He gave Michael a teasing wink.

"You ... oh, never mind." Michael closed his eyes and whispered, "Myriad."

The tingling began and the light enveloped him. Once the transformation was complete, he looked at Silas, his mouth and eyes agape. Finally, he said, "My God. That was—well, if a drag queen could do that, what a fucking show stopper that would be!" Then, he eyed Michael's costume and remarked, "It's pretty clear you inspired Melodie. That costume is ... mmmm. You can rescue me anytime."

Michael felt his cheeks go hot. "Okay, horny old man. Dial it back. It's not that kind of show."

Silas snapped his fingers. "Damn it!"

TWENTY-EIGHT

POSSIBILITIES

The next morning, Michael checked out of his hotel in Hell's Kitchen and took the subway down to Greenwich Village. He emerged from the Christopher Street-Sheridan Square station and made the short walk to the Stonewall.

He stood across the street from the Inn, which was now barricaded behind a wall of plywood. Power saws and hammers could be heard busily working at reviving the landmark. Unlike a lot of construction barricades, this one was emblazoned with the colors of the rainbow and the message: *The Stonewall—Sometimes you just need a facelift.* Underneath was a tentative opening date of late October.

He crossed the street and got closer to the barricade. Underneath the huge heading, there was a list of donors that had helped fund the repairs. He took in the names of those who had contributed to bring the Inn back to life. As he scanned the list, he saw a name that took him by surprise: *Travis Beauvais.*

He pulled out his cell phone and found Travis's number. He'd kept in touch with Slade's boyfriend since July. *So*, he texted, *I see your name on the list of people helping to fund Stonewall's revival. Good for you!* He added an applause and smiley face emoji.

Travis texted back: *I can't make up for what happened to my great uncle, but I can certainly honor his memory and keep the place that was so important to him—and all of us, really—alive. How are you?*

Michael replied: *Doing good. Just ready to head home after visiting Silas. I'll fill you in later.*

Travis then texted: *Are you flying home ...? Or are YOU FLYING home?*

Michael grinned. *I'll never tell!*

Travis replied with a winking emoji.

Michael found a nearby bench and took a seat. He had flown to New York City the way he always had via airliner. He honestly hadn't even thought about flying here as Myriad. He wasn't sure he would even have the power to fly that great a distance.

But Marcel had told him the glitches he'd experienced with Myriad's abilities before were over.

He unzipped his backpack and looked at the pendant. He noticed a folded piece of paper next to it. When he pulled it out, he realized it was Marcel's spell that had been inside the purse he'd returned to Silas. The old guy must have managed to slip it into his backpack when he wasn't looking.

He unfolded it and looked at Marcel's writing from all those years ago. The sun was beaming bright, making it easy to read. Then, Michael thought he caught something underneath the writing. He held the paper up to the sunlight, moving it slightly back and forth. Sure enough, there *was* something there. It looked like Marcel's script as well, but it was barely visible, as if he'd written it with invisible ink, or rubbed the words onto the sheet somehow.

Michael moved the paper around until the sun caught the hidden words just so. And his heart skipped a beat. He read it, only two words:

Be spectacular!

His heart ached to see Melodie again. But, as before, she'd somehow managed to reach out to Michael and say just the right thing. He looked up into the sky and pledged, "I'll do my best. I promise."

He returned the slip of paper to his backpack beside the pendant. The message inspired him. He walked around the Village for a while longer, taking in a few of the shops and buying a couple things. He had lunch in a small nearby café owned by a lovely gay couple. When he left the restaurant, he walked around to the alley behind it and ducked into a doorway to conceal himself from prying eyes.

He whispered, "Myriad." He hadn't used his powers since San Miguel. But Marcel's secret message felt like the permission he needed to move on and find out what this new life held.

He thought of one of the heroes he'd cosplayed with the gift of flight, and Myriad launched into the air, and then flew home toward Halifax.

He had no clue what the future had in store. But he was ready.

April 2022, Seattle, Washington